Aubrey's Innocence

By Bob Buckholz

PublishAmerica
Baltimore

ISBN: 1-60441-620-3
PUBLISHED BY PUBLISHAMERICA, LLLP
www.publishamerica.com
Baltimore

Printed in the United States of America

To Gloria

No one writes a book alone. There are many sacrifices made and research that is done. My mom, Barbara, helped immensely with the editing and story lines. It is still her inspiration that helps drive me.

Alyson Stinnett, for your amazing ability to edit my ignorance.

Jan stepped up for help on the book cover, posters for book signings, and her inspirational belief. With her hectic life, it was amazing that she could find the time. God Bless her, Jon and Nicole.

I'd also like to acknowledge Tim Isenberg, for his dedication to the Indiana State Police. It's amazing what you and your comrades do.

Also to my Creative Writing teacher at Alhambra High School in Phoenix, Arizona, you gave me the confidence to write the stories that reside in my head. My only regret is that I couldn't do it sooner or tell you about it.

Finally to my wife, Pam, your questions take me to the normalcy of the story. No matter how far out in left field I may say they are.

Chapter One

Aubrey sat in her dark room crying. Her legs were up, with arms folded around them. It was a position that she had gotten used to over the past few years, with her sobs being more of terror than sadness. She knew, as the night grew nearer, there would likely be another visitor, just like the one the night before. It was becoming harder for her to keep her poise for what her father called 'her uncles'. If she didn't act the way she was supposed to though, she believed the consequences would be worse than the acts themselves. It was those feelings that made her endure the pain and embarrassment of the visits.

She often thought, as she got older, the crying would fade away, and she would become immune to the constant barrage of abuse. She never did, and the crying never seemed to stop. She wiped her eyes and nose and looked out the window.

Aubrey always tried to make the walk home from school last longer. She sometimes stopped along the way to look into yards and walk slower as she got closer. Someone walking by, or a neighbor in their yard would sometimes speak to her as she stared into space. She would simply look at them with uncaring glances, and continue on her way. She heard them talking sometimes about how strange they thought she was, but that didn't matter to her. They didn't understand and never would.

It was cold outside, and the heat wasn't on in her house yet. Her father wasn't home to light the furnace, so the cold had worked its way through the walls of safety. She grabbed a blanket and covered herself. January was always cold, and this year snow lay on the ground. The moon was full, and the stars sparkled on the newly fallen white blanket. Her dad had to walk to work that morning because his car was buried in the driveway. His hangover had prevented him from getting the snow shovel out of the garage. She hated it when he walked. Walking meant she wouldn't hear him until the door opened. Worse was that he may get a ride from someone. Sometimes he would invite the driver in for a drink. The drink would mean later that night she would probably become the return favor for bringing him home.

Tomorrow she would be seventeen. There were no plans for a party, or even recognition of the day. She looked at the two posters she had on her walls, older ones that showed *KISS* and *Bon Jovi* early in their careers. The two posters she had in her room were there because of her friend Amy; she had given them to her when she got new ones. She wished she could fly away to their side of the world. Fantasy always helped her in these times. With a short trip in her mind she could dream and keep her spirits up.

She hadn't received a gift from her father since the day her mother left. She made gifts for herself, and wrapped them as if they were real presents. Sometimes she would take money from her father's dresser and buy herself a card and mail it to herself. She would grab it out of the mailbox before her father got home, and read it with the enthusiasm of a real birthday card.She dreamed of the day when she would be on her own, have a family, and shower them with love and adulation she should have gotten when she was young.

Aubrey's Mother had left three years ago. She remembered because it was only two days before her birthday when her parents decided to divorce. Aubrey believed her mother left because of something she had done, something that made her mother mad. She didn't believe her father when he told her she left because of infidelity. Every birthday would now be her reminder that she had caused her mother's departure. For whatever reason, she was the one at fault. Her father had never let her forget that day, the fight, the yelling, and then the finality of her mother walking out the door.

Her mother had accused him of cheating, accusations of running around with other women. He had denied it, but Aubrey knew it was probably true. She had come up to her room and told her to pack a bag, that the two of them were going away for a long time. When Aubrey finished packing, she went to her bedroom door just in time to see her father hit her mother in the face. He told her no one was going to take his daughter, and that he would kill both of them before he would let that happen.

Her mother came back into her room with a promise to her that she would be back. She said she would bring the police, and everything would be fine. She kissed her, then hugged her hard, took her bags, and headed down the stairs to a waiting taxi. Aubrey cried so hard that night she thought her eyes would fall out. It was the saddest day of her life.

Aubrey longed for her mother to return, to rescue her was more fitting. Her promise had to be real; it had to be because it was the only thing that gave Aubrey hope. That promise was the only thing that allowed her to dream. Her mother's return was the whole reason for living. The little time she had to herself, she would look out the window at other children with their mothers. They were playing in the street, walking the dog, or just hugging each other. Mothers weren't supposed to leave, they were supposed to stay and take care of their daughters.

Since her mother had left, her father had fallen into the clutches of booze. He would drink from the time he got home until he couldn't stand up any longer. He would eventually fall down on the couch, in a chair, or sometimes on the floor. Sometimes, Aubrey could hear him yelling into space, or blabbering about how Aubrey was too demanding, and her mother just couldn't take that demand anymore. He would be sprawled out in the morning when Aubrey got up and got ready for school. She wouldn't want to wake him, so she would carefully step over him. If he woke up, it would mean having to help him up or getting him breakfast. Smelling the remnants of the previous night's booze and cigars sickened her. It was that smell that kept her silence so deafening.

Before her mother left, they had a great family, or at least she thought so. They would always give each other a peck on the cheek, like they did on some of the old shows that were on cable. They were her favorite shows. She was in love with the way it used to be, and dreamed of how life would change when she grew up and met a man like the ones in the shows. She wished with all her might they could be a family again.

Three years is a long time when you're coming into adulthood. She longed for her mother to brush her hair and tell her stories at night while Aubrey danced her way into dreamland. She still hoped she would come back, but something inside told her it probably wouldn't happen. Her mother had virtually disappeared after she left. Neither Aubrey, nor her father had heard from her. Aubrey's father had expected some correspondence after the divorce. Weeks went by, then months, and now years. Aubrey had worried at first that something happened to her. Maybe she was dead, or had amnesia, something like that. Her friend Amy had done a search on the Internet and found nothing, except a woman with the same name going through nursing school. Eventually both Aubrey and her father lost hope and continued on with their lives.

Her father worked hard the first six months after her mother left, even with the drinking. He tried hard to have dinner ready, and all the laundry done, and Aubrey would help him clean the house. He didn't talk much at first, but once they got to know each other, you know the way kids and dads do, he opened up a little and told her what it was that took her mother away.

"She was always jealous," he told her. "She thought I was cheating, but I never did. Then she started getting jealous of you, of how I would play with you in the yard and things like that. She got worse as the years went along, so she took off."

Aubrey wasn't sure at the time what he meant by cheating, but Amy told her at school it was when he was having 'sex' with someone else, instead of his wife. Amy said cheating was a sin God wouldn't forgive, no matter what. She wasn't sure if her father was cheating then, but she knew he wasn't now. He never left the house, except to go to work or the liquor store.

Mrs. Williams, who lived across the street, would come over once a week, get some money from him, and go to the grocery store.

Sometimes, she would take Aubrey with her, and she would ramble on about all kinds of things that Aubrey didn't understand, or want to for that matter.

She got off of her bed, walked over to the window, and looked down on the street. The street lamp reflected off of the snow, and a small dog ran by the house. There was no one in the driveway yet, so she went back to her bed and sat down on the edge.

She picked up a brush and started to comb her long blonde hair. It wasn't clearly blonde like it used to be; it was kind of turning sandy blonde now. Amy said it was normal for a girl when she got older to have her hair change some. Amy had red hair, and she said that would never change, she was cursed with it for the rest of her life.

As she brushed her hair, she remembered it was about six months after her mom left Aubrey met her first uncle. Her father had been on an all weekend binge, and he was watching football on their television. He was yelling every once and a while at the refs or one of the players on the other teams he didn't like. A ring at the front door brought her out of her room, and she sat on the top stair to see who was there. Her father opened the door, and a tall man came into the house.

It hadn't occurred to Aubrey anything would have to do with her. He was just a friend of her father's and they were going to drink the night away. Both laughing and telling each other lies. Aubrey went back to her room to read a book for school, not thinking anything about the man or her father. The two would get drunk and the man would eventually leave. Her father would pass out in his chair and the night would be over. He didn't usually have anyone over to the house, so Aubrey thought he was a bit of a loner. However, tonight this man and her dad were having quite a time. She could hear them laughing and telling jokes over the loudness of the television. It seemed the only time it got quiet was when one or the other would go to the kitchen for another beer, or one of them would head for the bathroom.

The bathroom was upstairs, just down the hall from her room. It was small and cramped, and Aubrey could hear one of them stumbling up the stairs, fumbling for the doorknob, and then splashing their way through the ritual of peeing. She always thought it was gross how men had to pee. Standing up wasn't near as neat, and they always left the lid up, so she would have to put it down. That grossed her out.

Her father never checked on her at night. She would do her homework or color some in a book, and then she always wrote in her diary about the day she had. Then, she would put her diary away and get her bed ready. That always happened about 9 o'clock. She would lie down and drift into dreamland, where she could be whatever she wanted to be.

That night the man had come to her smelling of booze and bad after-shave. He forced his way into her bed and made her do things she knew nothing about. He told her to be quiet or he would hurt her, so she did what he asked and felt the guilt eat at her from that day forward. She didn't know then, her father had told him it would be all right if he went to her bed. The two drunken men had joked about it afterwards, making fun of her inexperience and inability to fight him off.

She was forced back into real time as she heard her father unlock the front door and come in stomping his feet. He had walked home, so Aubrey let out a small sigh of relief. Maybe tonight she would get a reprieve because of the cold weather and snow. She went to the door and listened as he worked his way into the kitchen and opened a beer. She heard him fixing himself something to eat and the television came on with the volume going up to a roar. She turned and went back to her bed, lying down on top of the covers.

She wished sleep would come as easy as it did before her mother left. It was hard to sleep anymore until she was just too tired to stay awake. She kept an eye on the door, expecting the worst to come through it at any minute. If she did dose off, she would come full awake whenever there was the slightest noise.

Tonight there was no knock on the door. There was no uncle to please. The later it got the better she felt. She drifted off to sleep with the sound of the television downstairs blaring away. It wasn't late yet, but it got dark so early in the winter and that made her so tired. Her last thought before sleep filled her world was her father must have been going deaf.

It wasn't that Ben Hendrickson was going deaf; it was the voices he heard with the television down low that kept him turning the volume up louder. He had heard the voices since his wife had left him, always trying to tell him what to do and when to do it. He succumbed to the voices sometimes, but he tried hard to ignore them for the most part. He knew he was eventually going to go completely insane, that is if the alcohol didn't kill him. Tonight the voices were very loud, and he was having a hard time making them quiet in his head.

"You're a man you imbecile. You have the right to happiness. Go upstairs and demand what she gives so freely to the other men. Go upstairs and demand it now!" his inner voices told him.

Ben sat and shook his head back and forth in the acceptable sign for no. He didn't want to climb the stairs, go into his daughter's room, and demand sex from her; he didn't want to be known as one of them. But she didn't even protest to the other men he sent up to her. She never screamed or yelled or refused. He thought he should be able to enjoy her too.

"That's right. Go up and tear her blankets off and jump on top of her. Have your way with her, she probably wants it," the voices continued.

Ben got up and started up the stairs quietly; trying not to make any noise that might alert her that he was on his way. He could be quiet, very quiet. He used to be quiet like this when he snuck home from a long poker game when he was married. He got to the top step and forgot it had a loud creak when you stepped on it the right way. It sounded like someone had set a timer off or dropped something, and he drew his foot up in haste, trying to make the noise go away in his head. He stood there for a few moments to make sure Aubrey wouldn't come out of her room.

Aubrey was drifting between the spot where sleep is in your head and reality is lurking just outside. She could hear what was going on, but it took a couple of seconds to realize it was the noise from the stairs that she heard. She jerked her head toward the door to listen for any more noise. She had her eyes wide open, trying to get as much light into them as she could. She took her blankets off quietly and swung her legs to the side of the bed. She stood up slowly and shuffled over to the corner of the room. Kneeling under a shelf her mother had put up for her dolls a few years back, she waited for the door to open.

Ben slowly walked to the door and turned the knob. He pushed the door open with just a slice of light showing into the room. He drew it back to him, and started to walk away, and go to his room. He hadn't slept there for so long, he couldn't remember if he would be able to sleep in the bed or not.

"C'mon you chicken shit," the voices came back. "She's almost a woman now. Get with it. All you do for her. She owes you."

He opened the door one more time; this time enough to see she wasn't in her bed. Aubrey was gone and the surprise made him sling the door wide open. Where was she, where could she have gone he thought to himself?

"Aubrey," he whispered.

There was no answer from inside the room. All that came out of the room was a blast of cold, winter air from the window. He went over to it and looked out. Nothing was in sight, only the bright snow reflecting off of the street lamp. He turned, went back out of the room, and down the stairs. He threw open the front door and looked out into the night. He saw the footprints in the snow leading away from the house. He had forgotten that he had walked home, and the prints were probably his from earlier. He shut the door hard on its hinges, and went back into his living room. He felt like another beer. Let the little bitch freeze, he didn't care.

Aubrey got up from under the shelf and went quickly to her closet. She put on her warmest clothes, and put on some black stockings and a jacket over her nightdress, thinking they would help her stay warm. She wasn't going to put up with this anymore; no one was going to use her like she had been used all this time. It seemed to her that her father was now going to start using her as a plaything, instead of just passing her around to whomever would pay or get drunk enough to talk him into letting them. Aubrey was determined that this wasn't happening to her.

Aubrey thought about all the men he had brought home to use her, to take advantage of a young girl. How could a father feel hatred so badly he would sell his own daughter? She was starting to get furious at the thought of all the times it had happened over the past three years. She was shaking with anger, fear, and loathing all at the same time, hating every one of those men, and her father. She had to do something about all of it; all of the bad had to turn into good.

She made up her mind that she would start to take care of herself, for good, and if that meant leaving this house, then she would go. She would pack some things and go somewhere. Anywhere was better than this, and she would make her plans from there. She had plenty of stops to make before it all would end. There were plenty of visits to make before she was finished. She finished packing and grabbed her diary, and her backpack, and slowly started down the stairs.

Unlike her father, Aubrey knew every loose board, every noise that the stairs would make as you went down them. She turned to her left when she was at the bottom and slipped by the entrance to the living room, moving toward the back door of the house. She could hear the television volume up in what seemed as high as it would go, knowing her father was plopped down in front of it, wondering where she had gone. She could see him in her mind's eye sucking down another beer and throwing it next to his chair. She didn't know why he had come up to her room, but she had a good idea. She put it in her head that it was the end of her staying quiet, the end of her years of abuse from all her father's friends. Those dirty, disgusting men he liked to call her "uncles". He had finally succumbed to the desire and decided he would try her out too; something Aubrey told herself long ago she would not allow. He had tried and now he would sit in his self-pity and squalor and try to rationalize his behavior.

She wasn't sure where she would stay that night, but wherever it was, it had to be better than where she was now.

She walked around to the front of the house and looked across the street at the Williams' house. She couldn't go there, but she could go over and tell Mrs. Williams where her husband had been some nights. She could go over and tell her what her husband had been doing while she slept. She decided that wouldn't be a good idea. There were other things she could do to get back at Mr. Williams, many things, things that would be far worse than embarrassment from their wives, or possibly divorce.

She decided that somewhere else would be more appropriate to stay, and far less dangerous to her.

Chapter Two

Darkness settles quickly in the hills of Tennessee, during January. Tim Williams could never get used to the early retreat of the sun. There always seemed to be things left to do after dark. He worked later in the winter than he ever did in the summer. During the winter months once five-o'clock reached the front door, so did the two mechanics that worked for him.

Tim owned and operated Williams Auto Repair. It was a small shop located just off Gay Street in downtown Knoxville. He'd been there since the early eighties, renting the same building from the same landlords. He had thought of buying the building, but the landlords always put him off. Part of Tim's problems with the landlord stemmed from his insatiable desire to gamble his earnings away. What little money was left, he drank into oblivion. It was always a race between the drink and the landlord as to who got the rent first.

His father was a drunk. His grandfather had been the same way. Tim figured that he wasn't going to be the one that broke the string of drunks in the family. Besides, Tim didn't have any children, only an overweight, nagging wife, that didn't want anything else but for Tim to stay at work. She could watch her soap operas during the day, and game shows at night. He cursed cable television with the new *"Game Show Network"*. Bringing those smiling talking heads into his living room every night, with all of their gleaming smiles, and perfect hair. What a bunch of pussies, is what he thought.

Tonight was going to be one of those long nights. Work came hard and the light of day would come too soon. He had promised his customer that her car would be ready by morning, and even though he may have been a drunk, he was good to his customers. It was the only thing that kept him in business. He was a very good mechanic, and there wasn't anything on a car, that he couldn't fix. He was a natural; at least that's what his customers told him. It wasn't easy either. So many things changed in the automotive industry since he opened his doors. Cars used to be a 'figure it out' sort of puzzle. Now you plugged them in and let the computers tell you what was wrong. He melted into the cars as they progressed, and that made him a sought after commodity in these parts. If Tim Williams said it was wrong, it was. If he told you he'd have it done by a certain date, you could bank on it, that's what made his services sought after in the city.

Today had been especially hectic at the shop. When it snowed things seemed to go wrong a lot more often than when there was nice weather out. He was convinced cars hated the cold as much as he did; after all he had a hard time starting in the morning too, just like a car. The weather seemed to make smaller things go wrong. So the day was spent with quick fixes on cars that either rolled in off the street, or were towed in by some of the services he had arrangements with.

He walked out of his office, and surveyed the shop for what he would need on the car in question. He pulled the jack over, and put the car up as far as he could with stands under all four corners. Even after that little bit of work, he got winded, and almost decided to go home and forget about the promise. He lit a cigarette, and looked at the old four-door Chevy he was going to work on. He couldn't walk away from it, as hard as he tried; he knew he needed to get it finished. He grabbed his creeper and put it next to the front of the car.

Tim wasn't a big man, but he was fairly tall and lanky. He had started to grow in certain areas over the past few years. His belly was starting to stick out a little more than he liked, and his chest seemed to be disappearing just as fast. He was considered to be tall, he guessed, at least taller than most of his friends. His hair was thinning, at least on top of his head, and it seemed to be getting thicker on his back. This was something his wife never let him forget.

He had also developed a cough in the last few months that was nagging to say the least. It seemed every time he would get busy with something, then the cough would hamper that progress. He thought the cigarettes were probably the cause. He didn't want to go to the doctor. He thought that might scare him too much to find out what the real cause was. So he stayed away, and he kept smoking. The coughing really started getting in the way when he made his visits to Ben Hendrickson's house.

Ben was his drinking partner at least that was the excuse he used most of the time when he went there. Tim often stopped over at Ben's after a hard day. He lived across the street, and the two had become friends, as well as neighbor's years ago. They weren't real close until Ben, had invited him over a couple of years ago, soon after his wife had left him. Tim thought it was some sort of comfort to sit and talk, and go over things of the day. At the end of the first evening he was there, Ben had introduced Tim to his young daughter. She was a beautiful girl with flowing blonde hair and bright blue eyes.

Tim had never wondered about young girls before, but after several nights of drinking and telling each other lies, Ben had offered his daughter as company to him. He reluctantly paid him the price. The reluctance he experienced was only for the first time he was with Aubrey. He enjoyed the girl, and over the years had made his visits to her home frequently. He forked over the cash to her father, and hiked up the stairs for his fifteen minutes of leaving all his worries behind. His fifteen minutes of being the big shot he always wanted to be. He could use his power on the girl, or be as nice as he wanted to be, it didn't matter. She would always do what he wanted her to do. Downstairs her father would sit in the living room and turn up his television. He acted like the noise from the TV would drown out the guilt he must feel for selling his only child to someone.

Tim would finish and come down, let himself out, and go back to his bitchy wife across the street. Sometimes he would sit and have another beer with Ben. It seemed as though Ben would change a little after the meetings with Aubrey, so Tim would normally only drink one beer, and then head for home. He knew it was wrong at first, but as Aubrey neared the age of consent, he justified the acts to himself with some sort of reasoning. It was all he needed.

A couple of months ago Tim stopped going to the house to see Ben or take the time with his daughter. He thought he had simply got bored with her, or maybe it was some sort of belated guilt that made him go on his way. It was during one of the visits the coughing had got so bad he had to leave early.

He would still stop over and see Ben sometimes, and Aubrey would come down the stairs to see who was there. Tim thought it was to make sure he wasn't coming up to visit with her, because she would look at him with contempt, and immediately go back up to her room. There was never any indication she even knew Tim. He soon stopped going to Ben's house, and they only saw each other if Ben brought his car into the shop for some sort of problem.

He suddenly needed a drink; these memories always brought that on. He needed a drink badly, before he started on this car. He went over to the dirty refrigerator that stood alone in the corner and got him a beer, opened it, and downed it in what seemed like two swallows. He grabbed another one and took one drink, then put it down on the workbench. He grabbed the creeper, and got down on his knees, laid down on it, and wheeled his body halfway under the car.

He looked around under the car at the different things he needed to work on, and to see what tools he needed. Suddenly he heard the front door of the shop open and close, and footsteps come around the car. He yelled while still looking at the underside.

"We're closed," he said. "If you need something, come back in the morning or wait, and I'll be out in a second."

He no longer had the words out of his mouth when he noticed a beautiful set of legs standing along side the car. They were wrapped in dark stockings with small healed, black flat-soled shoes on her feet. Gorgeous he thought; he even considered he might have said it out loud. Sometimes he wasn't sure if he did that or not. The legs started to the front of the car, stopping at the creeper.

Tim tried to see the woman's face through the open hood above, but she wasn't leaning over the car, she was just standing there.

"Take your time," she mumbled to him. "I've got all night."

Tim took the rag he had in his pocket and, wiped his dirty face. If he was going to come out from under the car, he wanted to at least look somewhat presentable for someone with nice legs like those. When he was finished, he slid the rag back into his pocket, and put both of his hands on the front bumper to pull himself out from under the car.

Just as he reached and grabbed the underside of the bumper to pull himself out, he felt the first blow to his left hand. There was a splitting sound of heavy metal crashing down on flesh against the chrome on the bumper. Before he could even yell the hammer came crashing into his right hand, hard and with such force he felt two of his fingers leave with a tear. The pain was so great he couldn't scream, or make any sound at all. He just lay there with his mouth open and no sound coming out. Both his arms dropped to his sides. He instinctively tried to bring them to his mouth, but found the hammer coming down hard again on each hand, two or three times on the left, and then the right. In just a few seconds his hands were useless to him, they laid motionless at his sides, with blood coming from every cut she had put there.

The next blow was to his legs, not just one blow, but a series of hits to the same area. Alternating hits again from left to right, striking his knees several times. Tim tried to raise his head to see, but smacked the underside of the car, and he fell back. He was screaming now, he could hear it, his hands and arms unable to move, with his legs throbbing with pain.

He saw her move away from the front of the car, and go to the side where he could hear her sliding the jack he had placed there back to the front of the car. When she had it in position, it went up and lifted the car a few inches off of the jack stands.

It was then he saw her face, as she bent down, and looked under the car. She had a cynical smile on her face, sort of a smirk, and her blonde hair coming down in front of her eyes. She brushed it back away, and reached in to get one of the jack stands that held the car in the air. She pulled it out, and then went to the other side of him to retrieve the other stand. She pulled it free from next to him, sliding it across the floor with a scrape.

Tim couldn't say anything, he couldn't move, the pain rushing through his entire body. He thought he recognized the woman's face, but couldn't quite put her name to it. He reached one more time with his battered hands to try, and pull himself out from under the car. When he did, pain flooded his senses and he dropped his arms once more. He couldn't move at all, she had made it impossible to grab and pull himself out, or even scoot along with the creeper.

She was standing directly in front of the car once more, next to the jack that was now holding the front of the car in the air.

"Always remember me," she said in a soft voice. "Always remember the innocence you stole."

With that, Tim saw the jack handle twist just enough for the pressure to lessen, and the car to start down. Panic replaced the pain, and he tried with all his might to lift his arms, and pull himself free. He couldn't move as the car came down, crushing his belly and chest first, and then his head. He lay motionless under the car, life slipping away with every second that went by. He knew he was dying, and the only thought he could muster as his last breath left him was, "damn, I need another beer".

The car sat without any movement. She walked around it one more time to make sure her prey would not be able to writher from his death bed. She took the jack out from the front of the car, and moved it to the back, parking it next to the rear bumper.

She saw the beer he had left on the bench, reached for it and took a long drink, then with her gloved hand; put it back where it was. Beer had never tasted so sweet to her. So sweet it almost was like sipping expensive champagne.

She went over to the trashcan and looked inside. It had been emptied at the end of the day so nothing was inside. She reached down and removed her shoes, then her stockings that were now spattered with the blood of the man she had just killed. She put the stockings in the can and lit a match, throwing it in with the stockings. The nylon burned quickly, curling up into a ball. Until it just disappeared at the bottom of the can.

She went to the front of the car one more time, and looked at the carnage she had just created. There was no movement from under the car; the blood was now starting to flow in a small river to the drain in the middle of the room.

She knelt next to the battered legs, and took a rose from her cleavage, placed it between his legs and stood back up.

"Remember me, remember the innocence you stole," she repeated once more.

She turned, and walked out the door. There was no remorse, no looking back, and it had been easy, even if it was the first.

Chapter Three

Detective Ryan Rose was in his family room, playing with his new baby boy. He was on his back on the floor with him on his chest. Every few seconds, he would throw him up in the air, catching him as he came down. At six-months old, it was a game that got both of them laughing hard. The enjoyment it gave to Ryan was indescribable. The play was allowed because he woke up early this morning, and he was going to let his wife Laura, sleep a while longer.

The phone rang in the other room, and if he had learned anything in his eight years on the force was that when the phone rings early, the criminals were probably busy the night before. He got up and carried his son with him to the kitchen.

"Detective Ryan," he answered.

The dispatcher on the other end of the line informed him that the Chief of Detectives wanted him to pick up his partner, and after he did, to call him as soon as possible. Ryan hung up the phone, and started to his bedroom. He put his son in bed with his wife, and got dressed for the day. Their little boy immediately cuddled next to his mother.

They had been married only three years, and Laura hadn't yet gotten used to early calls, and the concern that goes along with being a cop's wife. She never said much, but Ryan could see the worry in her eyes when he was called unexpectedly. He tried to be quiet and not wake her, but when Josh moved on the bed, it woke her up. She rolled over, and looked at Ryan while he was dressing. He hesitated for a moment, and looked at his wife. She was beautiful, even in the morning, when she only had her fresh morning face on. She was on her back, with Josh cuddling next to her, trying to get as close to his mother as he could. She instinctively put her arm around him, picking him up just a bit in a protective manner. Ryan had a fleeting thought about how lucky he was.

"I thought you started your vacation today," she said sleepily.

"The office just called and they need me for a while this morning," he said, as he gave her a kiss on her forehead. "I'll try not to be too long, ok?"

Ryan didn't give her a chance to respond as he put his gun in his shoulder holster, and slipped his jacket over the black turtleneck he was wearing. He kissed Laura one more time, and gave Josh a hug as he settled back to sleep next to his mother. He grabbed his cell phone and headed out the door.

When he got into his car Ryan took his phone out, and called into the office. He needed to see if they had called his partner, or if it was going to be a surprise to him to pick him up on the way in. The morning cold crept into his bones as he listened to the ring of the phone on the other end. The snow was a lot deeper than it was when he had gotten home, and getting out of the garage was a bit of a task. He backed down the drive and headed up the street, sliding to a stop.

"Have you contacted Detective Breeding?" he asked the dispatcher when she came on the line. "You have, good I'll swing by and get him on my way in, thanks," he hung up.

Ryan lived on the northwest side of Knoxville. His home was just off the interstate everyone called the Pellissippi Highway, named for the college that is located on the north end of Interstate 295. It was a loop around the city that never really looped. It simply went as far as exit 11 and stopped just north of Maryville, Tennessee. His partner Don Breeding lived in a small farm house not far from the exit, so it was a little out of the way. Ryan hoped the snowfall last night wouldn't make it too difficult to get in his driveway.

Ryan was used to going and getting Don, because half the time his car was broken down, and the other half he had lent it to someone he had met the night before, and they hadn't returned it yet. He was a good partner and a great humanitarian. He was just a horrible judge of character. Three of his cars had been picked up by the department this year alone, either abandoned on the side of the road, or crashed with some drunk behind the wheel, asleep or passed out.

They had been partners for two years now, Ryan knew him while he was a beat cop, but not very well. The two had made detective close together, and so the Chief of Detectives felt they would do fine as partners, once they got their feet wet working with more experienced detectives. They both spent their rookie year with seasoned detectives, and then were assigned to homicide, and partnered up.

He pulled up into Don's driveway and honked his horn lightly. Don came out still trying to get his jacket on, and his holster, and gun in his hand. He looked like he hadn't slept that night, his hair still ruffled, and eyes so red Ryan could see them from the car. He wasn't a tall man, but had prided himself on how much muscle he could pile on his arms and legs when he was younger. When they were beat cops, there were rumors the department had to order special uniforms to fit his upper arms. Ryan chuckled lightly as Don struggled to get his jacket over his shoulders while moving toward the car. At one point it looked like he would slip on the snow, but he steadied himself as he finally made it to the front seat.

He hadn't been into lifting weights for a few years now, so his mid section was starting to suffer from too much fast food, and not enough fast exercise. It had become a quiet joke around the office. Not a great deal was made of it because most knew if they got him in the wrong mood, those arms and legs could still be harmful, no matter how big the belly was.

Don slid into the car, and finished stowing his gun under his arm.

"Morning, I'll bet you were glad to hear from the office this morning. I thought you were supposed to be in Cabo or somewhere like that?" he said with a slight sarcasm. "Where we going, what are we doing?"

Don always like to tease or ride Ryan about being tied down to one woman, and especially about having a kid, "won't have any more fun now that the kid's here," he had told him several times.

"I don't know yet, they called me and told me to pick your lame ass up, and call into the office. Chief Sammons wants to see us. You can imagine Laura is real happy, we're supposed to be on vacation this week."

"Chief huh, must be something important, you know he wouldn't call out his favorite detective for nothing," he chuckled again, and made a face that looked ridiculous.

Ryan took his phone out again, and dialed the Chief of Detectives. Whatever had gotten everyone out of bed so early, had to be something that made the papers that morning. The chief didn't call for just any run of the mill crime in the city.

Knoxville is a small city that's trying to become a large one. The center of the city is housed on the Tennessee River, which at one time was the main center of revenue for the inhabitants. Since the University of Tennessee, and it's football team had come along, the river was now used more for those that couldn't get tickets to the games, or the whims of politicians that used it for recreation, and showing off to out of town guests.

In the center of town, there was a large gold glass ball, which sat on top of a single rising column. It resembled a huge golf ball, rising out of the buildings around it. Residents that had been there for years knew it was part of the World's Fair in the early eighties, while some new residents thought it was just an eye sore of a failed attempt to revive the downtown area. If you were in the downtown area, you could see the ball from just about anywhere you went.

Its people are a diverse group divided by the rich, the poor, and the rest. The rich live predominantly on the west side in what's known as Beardon, and other suburbs created by the dot com boom, or in outlying smaller towns. The poor in the middle, and surrounding suburbs, and then the rest are sprinkled around into other small communities, and in the Great Smoky Mountains, located to the east of the city. Crime hasn't learned to catch up with Knoxville yet. Sure, there are murders and robberies, but it's nowhere near as bad as other cities of the same size. When there is a bad situation it becomes a part of the heart of everyone in East Tennessee, not just Knoxville. It seemed as though the people of the surrounding area take serious crime somewhat personal, and so they were always interested when something big hit the media.

Ryan knew if he was being called off vacation, this crime was one of those that would turn the papers inside out, and be the lead story on every television station in town. By noon, everyone in the city, and surrounding area would be talking about it. The south is just that way. No secrets and lots of rumors.

The Chief of Detectives answered his phone as soon as it rang.

"Ryan, don't bother going into the office, there's a small auto repair shop just off of Gay Street on Vine," he paused for a short time. "I think it's called William's Auto or something like that, you won't miss it, there's a ton of ambulances and press cars out in front, meet me there."

The indication of the press being involved already was the telling story that whatever this was, it was big. Ryan turned off the highway and headed to the downtown area.

"We've got a hot one Don," he told his partner. "When we get there let me do the talking to the press, you simply keep with the head nod and no comment."

"Yes boss," and he responded with a sloppy military salute.

The two men knew exactly where the trouble was when they got on Gay Street, and saw a roped off area at the intersection of Vine. Cars and television crew trucks were parked everywhere, blocking the road completely. Ryan drove up as far as he could, then showed his badge to the officer on duty. He lifted the yellow tape, and Ryan drove the short distance to a small garage that was on the north side of the street. The Chief was already there with several other agencies, including the County Coroner. They parked in the middle of the street, and got out.

Immediately Ryan saw the blood had run from under the car that sat in one of the bays of the garage. It looked like a huge amount for one murder. The blood ran from under the car to a drain in the middle of the bay.

"They're getting ready to lift the car now," The Chief said.

"Why call us for a car falling on a mechanic?" Breeding commented more than questioned.

27

The three men went to the front of the car, and Ryan and Don saw this wasn't a simple car falling off of a jack situation. The man under the car had both legs beat almost where they were detached from his knees. Both of his hands and wrists were, mildly put, hamburger at the end of his arms. Someone had taken a real dislike to him, and made a point that he would hurt before they dropped the car on him.

Chief Bob Sammons started the conversation; "I got the call from one of his mechanics over there just after six this morning. Says the dead man's name is, Williams, he owns the place, and apparently was going to work on this car late last night. The mechanic says he left at five o'clock last night and everything was all right then. He waited outside for Williams, but when he didn't show, he tried the door and found him like this."

Ryan bent down and looked under the car. The man's chest and head were crushed by the weight of the car, next to him were the tools he was using at the time the car fell on him.

"They know yet how long he's been dead?" he asked.

"Coroner says he won't be able to tell much until they get him out from under there. He did say that with the rigor in his legs that it happened sometime last night. There wasn't any alarm or anyone that was supposed to come by last night after all his help left, so apparently there was no reason for anyone to come in until morning. We talked to the owner of the car a few minutes ago; they were supposed to pick it up this morning. One thing for sure, he pissed someone off, and it looks like they tortured him before they dropped the car on him."

Ryan turned, and told Don to grab another officer, and do some canvas of the area. There was probably not much anyone would have seen. This part of town wasn't the talking type, and once the lights go down, there isn't much to watch anyway, at least that you would want to talk about. Ryan reached into the man's pocket, and got his wallet. He opened it, and got his address off of his driver's license.

Timothy Williams was his name, and he lived not far from his garage.

"What do you think about the rose left there between his legs?" Ryan asked the chief. "Doesn't seem like a man would leave a rose, does it? Could we be looking at some sort of crime of passion here?"

"We're trying to find a next of kin now," Sammons said. "I guess it could be anything at this point."

Detective Breeding walked up on the two men bringing a uniformed officer with him and a small man dressed in old, clothing. He was dirty, and so were his clothes. He looked as though he was homeless. Don pulled Ryan to the side away from the car, and others listening.

"He says he heard a lot of screaming coming from inside last night, around seven o'clock," he told him. "Says it might have been a little later, he wasn't sure. He says he was on his way to the shelter, over by the bridge, when he heard the screaming."

"Is he sober Don?" Ryan asked. "He doesn't look as though he could remember much of anything."

"Says he'll never forget it as long as he lives, says it was the most horrifying screams he's ever heard."

"See if you can get him to pinpoint the time a little closer, and see if he remembers any cars around, or someone that may have looked out of place here last night."

Don went back over to the little man who was standing next to the refrigerator. Ryan watched him walk over, and noticed the half full bottle of beer on the workbench.

"Don, make sure someone gets that beer bottle and have it checked for fingerprints, or anything they can get off of it."

Chief Sammons came back over to Ryan, and stood face to face with him. The two were almost exact in height, but Sammons was much bulkier. Ryan thought he was probably the most intelligent human being he had ever met. His ability to work his people was beyond reproach, and respect wasn't something that came hard to him.

"The coroner says this guy has been dead for twelve hours or so. This was no accident Ryan, but of course you can see that. The press will be all over this, it's gruesome, and it's a murder that has some emotion to it. We need to find out everything about this guy, and whatever you find out you need to bring to me directly. Try to keep as much to yourself as you can for the time being. I've called the Chief of Police, and he'll call a press conference soon, so we need something as fast as you can find it out."

Ryan motioned to Don that it was time to leave. They would drive over to the dead man's house and see if there were a spouse, if so, they would deliver the bad news. A hell of a way to start your day, he thought to himself.

When the two of them got in their car, and started to drive away. Several reporters that were waiting tried to stop the car and get statements. Ryan saw one of the reporters he knew from other crime scenes, and stopped the car. He rolled down the window, and motioned for him to come over.

"Call me in a couple of hours," he told him. "I can't give you anything right now, but we'll see what's going on, and go from there."

The reporter nodded, and started to walk away when Ryan called out to him. The reporter turned around and came back, "you know that if you find something out, you need to let me know, right?"

This time the reporter didn't say anything, he just turned, and walked back to the yellow tape, he turned around when he got there, and just smiled at Ryan.

Ryan knew Sammons had told him to keep what he knew to himself. He read between the lines from him, and figured that the Chief wanted someone Ryan trusted to break the story. The way the department wanted it reported. Sure there would be others on it, and they would have some facts, but not the ones the department wanted released. He drove away slowly with a nod from his friend.

"You ready for a hell of a wake-up for someone?" he asked his partner. "I'd sure hate to start my day like this."

Chapter Four

Amy Temple was Aubrey's best friend in the world. The two had been through everything together. She was the only person Aubrey could talk to, and she was the only one Amy could share secrets with. Aubrey had never told Amy about the things she had to do at home, but everything else was trusted between both of them.

Amy looked at her friend sleeping on the floor next to her bed. She had shown up shortly after ten o'clock, freezing, and looking for somewhere to sleep. She said she had a fight with her father, and needed to stay the night. Amy's mother wanted to call her father, but Aubrey had begged her not too. Her mom gave up, and decided she would contact him in the morning, after the three of them had talked at breakfast.

It was shortly after eight, and the two were supposed to be up already, and getting ready for school. Aubrey had a restless night, so Amy decided to let her sleep a little longer. Now her mother was starting to call from the kitchen that breakfast was ready, and the two girls were going to have to get up.

Amy reached down, and gave Aubrey a gentle shake on the shoulder. She moaned softly, but didn't open her eyes. When she turned over some of the blanket moved on her shoulder, and Amy noticed two or three spots of blood on her skin. They weren't large, and they weren't scabbed, they were just dried blood. It creeped her out for a minute, but she really didn't think anything about it. She gave her another shake, and told her that she needed to get up.

Aubrey turned over on to her back, and looked up at her friend. Her eyes were swollen and red. She looked as though she hadn't slept at all.

"Where am I?" she asked Amy.

"Quit being silly, you're at my house, now get up so we can get ready for school, my mom's got breakfast ready and you know she wants to call your Dad."

Amy grabbed the blanket, and threw it back, exposing Aubrey's body to a sudden coolness.

"Give it back," she said with a whine. "I'll be late for school today, I have to go home and get some clothes."

She sat up quickly and looked at Amy, "you can't let your mom call my Dad, Amy, she just can't, do you understand, she just can't," she said pleading.

Geez, take it easy, let's go talk to her and see what to do. What do you mean you'll be late for school? You have to be on time, we have tests today, and what do you mean you have to go home and get clothes, where are you going?

Amy's questions came rapidly together, almost like she didn't dare take a breath, or think about what she was saying. She really sounded surprised at Aubrey's revelation about school today.

Despite Aubrey's problems at home, she had maintained a very high grade point average. She worked hard at each of her classes, and excelled in everything she did. She was President of the Debate Club, and worked easily with teachers, and other students. Her only social life consisted of walks with Amy, and an occasional movie. She never went to any parties, and had no interest in seeing boys, or dating at all.

Amy always thought it was a little strange that she wouldn't date. Some of the other girls that didn't know her had speculated she was a lesbian, but Amy knew that was crap, and defended her friend whenever the subject came up. Amy just figured she had no interest in men, and would develop that after she finished her studies, or after she graduated from college.

"I can't go to school with you today, Amy," Aubrey told her friend.

"I kind of ran away last night. I had a really bad fight with my dad, and I can't go home yet. I'm going to wait until he goes to work, and then go get some clothes."

"Where will you go?" Amy asked, "And how did you get blood on you?"

"I fell on the way over here last night; some kid's bike was in the way. I was hoping I could stay with you for a little while," she said wrinkling her brow, "I really don't have anywhere else to go."

The two girls sat and looked at each other for a couple of minutes. Amy knew her mom would probably freak, but there wasn't any choice. She decided they had to ask her to allow Aubrey to stay, and not tell her father where she was.

"We have to ask her, Aubrey, but you have to tell her the truth, you have to tell her you had a fight with your father."

"What if she asks what it was about? I can't tell her the reason, I can't tell anyone what it was about."

"Let's do this. You go to your house and get your clothes, and I'll go ahead and go to school. Come over after I get home and we'll talk to her then."

Aubrey and Amy both agreed it was the best plan to do it her way. Aubrey was terrified to go back to her house, but knew it had to be done. It was a good plan.

The two girls went to have breakfast with Amy's mother. It wasn't hard to get her to agree to what they had planned, after she knew there was trouble at home for Aubrey. She didn't know the whole story, but she knew enough that she wanted Aubrey to stay safe. After breakfast, Amy went with her mother to school, and Aubrey headed over to her house to get some things, and bring them back to the house.

She rounded the corner to her street, and saw there were police cars all around Mr. William's house, across from hers. She didn't think they would be there for her; surely her father wouldn't have called them because she ran away last night. He was too loaded when Aubrey snuck away to call anyone, so she wondered what the problem was.

She walked to her driveway, and started across to the front door. She tried to ignore all the police cars, and nonchalantly go into her house.

As she got to the door, one of the policemen across the street called out to her, and asked her to wait. He started across the street to meet her. She walked toward him, wondering why he would want to talk to her.

"Good morning, Miss. My name is Detective Ryan Rose; can we talk for a minute?"

Aubrey really wanted to run, but as she looked around she could see nowhere to go. She stopped, and the detective came to her with his hand extended to shake.

"Aubrey Hendrickson," she said with a smile.

"Do you live here Aubrey?"

"I guess you could say that," she said. "Right now I'm coming to get some clothes to go to my friend's house for a week or so," she continued.

"I hope everything is ok?"

"Just the normal teenager and father trouble, it's nothing we won't work through."

Aubrey wanted to stop the conversation, because she really didn't have time to idly chitchat with a policeman from across the street. Detective Rose obviously felt her discomfort, and continued with a more business like attitude.

"Do you know your neighbors across the street?" he asked, pointing to the house where all the cars were.

"Yes sir, Mr. and Mrs. Williams."

"Last night, Mr. Williams was killed in his shop downtown. We're investigating the case, and just talking with all the neighbors. We knocked on your door, but no one answered, are your parents home?"

She knew that if he had knocked too early her dad would have been passed out on the living room floor, so he wouldn't have come to the door. She looked at the detective for a moment.

"Mr. Williams wasn't a very nice man," she stuck her key in her door, "he had habits most would think a little strange," she said.

"What habits, Aubrey?"

"Let's just say he didn't have much of a love life with his wife, and leave it at that," she said with contempt.

"That's interesting you would bring that up. Your next-door

neighbor says you and Mr. Williams may have had some problems in that area."

Aubrey stared at the detective for a moment again. She had no idea any of the neighbors were aware of what went on with her and Mr. Williams. She suddenly felt ill, a sick feeling in her gut from knowing that a person knew what was happening, and didn't do anything to stop it. It was almost as bad as her father's participation in the whole matter.

"I have to get ready for school," she lied.

She opened the door, and stepped through, not giving the detective any time to object. She peered out the window, and watched as he walked back across the street. When he got to the middle of the street he stopped, turned back around, and looked at the house Aubrey was in. Aubrey peeked through the curtain at him, wishing under her breath he would go away. She said it over, and over again in her head, just keep walking, just go back to the other house and leave me alone. She felt like it was more of a prayer than her thoughts.

The detective turned back around, and then continued his trek to the other side of the street. After a couple of seconds, he disappeared back into Mr. William's house. Aubrey wondered how his wife took the news of her husband's death. They didn't seem to be very compatible to her, that's why he would come over to her to fulfill his desires, and drink with her father. He was an asshole, she thought to herself. Not only was he that way to her, but to his wife too. She probably put on the façade of being hurt by his death, but Aubrey wondered if his wife felt the same relief she did.

She turned, and started up the stairs to her room. She was afraid to look in the living room where her father spent so much of his time. He was supposed to be at work, but there was more than one day he called in sick when he woke up and realized it was noon, or he wouldn't bother to call at all. She stayed to the right of the stairs so if he was there, he wouldn't hear the creek of any of the old wood.

When she got to the top she turned to the right, and went by the bathroom. She took a quick look to the right thinking she would see the door closed, and simply move on to get her things. She got a completely different view.

The shower curtain was torn down from the clips. Some were still hanging, and pieces of the curtain still clung from the metal pole. There seemed to be something scrawled in a red substance on the mirror. She squinted hard to see if she could read it from where she was standing, but the angle was wrong, and she couldn't make out the writing. She looked down, and noticed the throw rug on the floor was soaked. There was water running from under the closed shower curtain that hid the bathtub. She hesitated to move the curtain back, and see what was in the tub. Slowly, she raised her hand, and took hold of the curtain, pulling it back slowly. She could see the water was trickling out of the faucet, and filling the tub. It must have run all night. She reached in without opening the curtain any further. She squeezed the cold water, but it was shut tight already, so she reached for the hot water handle. Just as she touched it a hand came from nowhere, and grabbed hers. She jumped backwards, taking the curtain with her as she fell to the floor. She was trying to get away from the curtain, rolling back and forth on the floor, as she tried to free herself.

Finally she was free, and she scrambled to her feet, pressing her back to the other side of the bathroom. She looked in the tub, and saw her father sitting there, naked from the waist up, a beer bottle in one hand, and the other hanging off the side of the tub. Bubbles were coming from his closed lips as he mumbled in an unidentifiable language. His hair was wet, and he looked as though he was trying to shower, but couldn't figure how to get the water to come out. She thought he must have been falling down drunk, and almost completely passed out.

She turned to leave the room, and simply leave him in the tub. She reached and turned the faucet the rest of the way off, then looked at the mirror. A tube of lipstick was lying in the sink, and scribbled on the glass was her name. Under it was simply written, "Revenge".

Aubrey stared at the mirror for what seemed forever. She finally got control of herself, and left the bathroom. She went to her room, and started to quickly pack what she thought she needed to stay with Amy for a few days. The message on the mirror didn't mean anything to her at the moment, but the longer she thought, the more it seemed like her father could not have written it, he was too far gone in his booze. Even with the abstract meaning, the message scared her. She felt as if she needed to get out of the house as soon as she could.

She went back downstairs and started back out of the house, but stopped. She felt as if she should get her father out of the water before she left, so he wouldn't drown. She went back upstairs, and tried to lift him out of the tub. He was heavy, but she managed to get him out, and place him on the floor. She turned him over on his side and started to walk out again.

When she got to the door he mumbled lightly under his breath, "she was here last night," and passed back out into his world of unconsciousness.

Chapter Five

Doctor Charles Cranston worked his putter back and forth on the carpet of his office, striking nothing but air. He loathed the winter, and yearned for spring to be sprung so he could hit the golf course again. He sat the putter directly in front of the ball, and took his best short putt. He struck the ball just hard enough to get it to the glass he had laid on its side ahead of him. The ball rolled smoothly across the carpet, and straight by the glass. Another miss, he thought to himself.

His phone beeped on his desk, and his nurse came on the line over the speaker, "Doctor, your next patient is here," she said, in her best operator voice.

He put the club back in his closet, and headed down the hall to his examining room. He was getting far too lax in his duties, his abilities weren't suffering, but his mind felt the boredom of the same old thing every day. He was in a rut, plain and simple. He felt as if it was time to make a call to his favorite playmate, maybe they could meet tonight, the visit seemed to always break the boredom of everyday life. He sure hoped so.

Of course his playmate was going back to school after the Christmas break. That shouldn't stop her from wanting to play a little "doctor" for a couple of hours tonight. He made a mental note to make sure to call her father after he was finished with his patient.

His nurse was coming down the hallway after taking vitals from his patient in the examining room. She was a plain woman, small and stocky, not quite fat, but plenty of meat on her bones. She had short hair and looked like a woman that you would think was a nurse. She fit the profile very well in her smock with baby elephants plastered all over it, and comfortable shoes on her feet.

She always had a smile on her face, and a joyful laugh, and a great sense of humor, which greeted everyone. He kept her in his office because she wasn't only proficient at her job; she made everyone around her happy, including him. It really helped with the patients, especially the younger ones, and the ones that were getting too old to appreciate life anymore. She was also very efficient with the everyday duty of keeping things in the office straight.

When she walked past the doctor she rendered a salute as if they were both in the military. Charles was looking down at the chart for the patient, and pretended not to notice what she did. She went on by and, as she did, he wiggled his butt at her, knowing she was looking back to see what he would do.

He walked into the examining room, and greeted his patient with as much gusto as he could muster. She was an older woman that looked as though she needed a drink worse than she needed a doctor. He took his stethoscope out, lifted the back of her blouse, and listened to her heart for a couple of minutes. He was just finishing when his receptionist broke in on the intercom.

"Dr. Cranston," she said. "I have someone on the phone that says it's an emergency, she needs to talk with you now, do you want to take the call?"

"Give me a couple of minutes, tell her I'll be right with her," he put the tool back, made his obligatory apologies and went into his office.

"Hello, this is Dr. Cranston," he said into the phone.

"Doctor, can you come over tonight to see my father, he's as bad as I've ever seen him," he thought he recognized Aubrey's voice on the other end.

"Of course, Aubrey, I would be glad to come over and see you, I mean your father. What do you want me to bring tonight?"

"Doctor, I'm serious, he's passed out on the floor of the bathroom and he's gurgling, and mumbling incoherently about something, I think this time it's really bad."

Charles gathered up his composure, and told the voice on the other end his last appointment was at three, and he would try to come over after that, "will you be there?" he asked her.

"If I'm not, you can come in the back door, he's upstairs right now, but I don't know what kind of shape he'll be in by the time you get there. I got him out of immediate danger; still I think he needs to see you."

Dr. Cranston was used to going to Ben Hendrickson's house, either to help him through another drunken night or as an "uncle" for Aubrey. She sounded as though she was really worried this time. He told her he would come for sure. It would mean putting off another golf game on the carpet, but what the hell. Ben had allowed him to have a lot of pleasurable nights, and besides, playing golf in your living room, wasn't near as fun as the real thing.

He finished with the patient, which took almost an hour, and told his receptionist to cancel any other patients he may have for the day. He wanted to go over to Ben's house, and get him straight before he killed himself on the bathroom floor, perhaps drowning in his own vomit. He got his coat, and headed out the door, his nurse voicing her displeasure with his decision to cancel the day as he went.

It was an especially cold day. The humidity was up making it feel a lot colder than it actually was. He couldn't remember a winter as cold as this in Tennessee. He remembered an ice storm that took everyone by surprise back in 1994, but this was different. There wasn't quite as much moisture in the air as back then. He got in his car, and drove to Ben's house. He noticed the police were just pulling away from a house across the street as he arrived. It intrigued him, but he dismissed it as a fleeting thought.

He walked up the front, and knocked on the door. There was no answer, so he walked around to the back as instructed on the phone. On his way, a neighbor stuck her head out of the door, and gave him a hearty wave hello. Doctor Cranston had treated almost everyone in the area at some time or another, so it wasn't unusual for him to see people that he knew all the time. He waved back, and went to the back where he found the door unlocked.

When he got inside he closed the door behind him, and immediately noticed there was water dripping from around the light in the kitchen.

He started up the stairs to see if someone had left the sink or tub running in the bathroom. He was familiar with the house from visits he had with Ben, and with Aubrey. He had often thought his obsession with Aubrey couldn't be normal, but he really did love her. His head told him it wasn't love unless she loved him back. In his case it was probable that it was infatuation with the young girl.

When he had first treated Ben's wife, Aubrey's mother, he had admired how intelligent their daughter seemed. She would read in the waiting room, and then sit and watch him do whatever it was her mother was there for. She would ask questions about some of the treatments, and she really seemed to understand when he would explain something to her. He hoped she would have the interest to become a doctor someday.

When he met Ben Hendrickson, it was to treat him for what Ben thought was depression. Charles had examined him, and found his depression came from a poor marriage more than anything. He prescribed a new anti-depressant, and told him to come back in a month. When he returned he told Charles his wife had left him, and Aubrey, and the medicine wasn't doing him any good. Charles felt a visit or two to his home would help cheer him up, so he visited a couple of times.

When he went to see Ben, the two started drinking some beers. Charles knew it was probably against what he thought Ben should do, but the stress it relieved for him was as important as Ben's. It was after several visits that Ben offered Charles the company of his daughter in return for forgiving a couple of the bills he had sent the family. His first inclination was, it was morally wrong, and it was certainly ethically wrong. He had also wrestled with the fact it was her father that was doing the encouragement. That fact baffled him more than anything. What would drive a man to sell his daughter, no matter what the price? Charles knew Ben was depressed, and had thoughts that there was no one left in the world for him. He was lonely, and the fact that someone would come to talk with him, meant a great deal to Ben. After denying the offer several times, the thought of being with the young girl soon became too much of a temptation, and he succumbed to his desires.

He had stressed with the guilt for weeks, but found the more he thought about it, the more he knew he had to be with her again, and again. It was a cycle he couldn't break.

He reached the top of the stairs and looked in the bathroom. The bathtub was running over the side, but there wasn't anyone in the tub itself. He reached over, and turned the water off. He felt the water under his feet as he walked, and could hear the squish of liquid moving from under his shoes as he went back into the hallway.

He thought Aubrey, had called, and said her father was sick, but he didn't seem to be around the house anywhere. He called out his name, but got no reply. He went back downstairs, and looked in the living room. The television was playing as usual, but the volume was turned down to where you could barely hear it. Charles expected to find Ben in this room, passed out drunk on the floor or sofa. He walked into the dining room, where dishes were piled on the table where no one ate anymore. Some looked as though they had been there for days, maybe even weeks. He continued his search in the kitchen and throughout the lower floor of the house.

Ben wasn't downstairs, so he must be upstairs. Charles called out his name again, and as he did, thought it was unusual Aubrey would leave and not be there with her father. He knew they had been having trouble, and he knew it was probably because of letting her be with him. She didn't understand that he really did love her, and if he could, he would take her away, and they could live happily ever after. It was all a dream, of course, but it was something he could run through his head like the fairy tale it was.

He topped the stairs again, and called out Ben's name one more time to no avail. He turned and went toward the bedroom Ben was supposed to be in. He knew he didn't sleep there much anymore, but if he were feeling bad, maybe he would crawl up to it, and get in bed, or perhaps Aubrey, put him there after she telephoned him.

The bedroom was empty, with no sign the bed was ever slept in. The doctor scratched his head with question. Why would she call him, and say her father was sick, then take him to the hospital? He shrugged his shoulders, and went down the hall to Aubrey's room. He looked in with a blank stare that told he was dreaming of her again. He turned and went back downstairs. When he rounded the corner, and headed toward the kitchen, he heard a whimper, just loud enough to catch his attention.

He was standing next to a door that led to the basement. Not many houses have basements in Knoxville, but this house was equipped with a nice finished area that hadn't been used in a long time. He and Ben had used it several times years ago when they would drink beer, and tell each other their stories. Ben was his release from the stuffy world of being a doctor. So many people to please and so many that only wanted to know you because of your profession. He would come over here when he longed for the fresh feel of just being himself. Charles opened the door, and heard the moan one more time, this time a little louder.

"Ben, is that you?" He spoke into the darkness. "Are you all right Ben?"

There was no answer to his question, so he went down the stairs, turning on the light as he went. The bulb in the stairway came on, but went out immediately with a pop. He continued down, and tried the light when he reached the bottom. There was no light, none in the stairs, or the room where a pool table sat idle in the middle. It was dark, but some light filtered through from the windows that were high above the floor. Charles could see there was no one on the floor, or on any of the chairs that sat around the room. Again he heard the moan, this time he pinpointed it coming from what was once a bedroom in the corner of the basement. He worked his way past the pool table, using it as a leaning post, and guide at the same time. He could feel the soft felt on the table, and kept his hand there for a second longer, just to get his eyes adjusted to the semi darkness.

He reached the door, and turned the handle slowly, opening the door with a loud creak from the rusty hinges.

In the middle of the room was an old bed. It had no headboard or footboard, and sat with only a frame, with no sheets or blankets. Ben was laying face down on the mattress, in a position that had to be uncomfortable, even for someone young. His arm was over his head, and his legs were crossed at the knee. It looked as though he had been thrown on the bed, or fallen as he attempted to negotiate a safe landing on it. He was half clothed, and looked as though he had one terrible night that had spilled over to the day.

"Ben," he said. "What the hell have you done to yourself now?"

He went to step into the room, and help Ben at least get to his feet, or get him where he could see him, and start the sobering up process. As he let go of the door, something hit him hard in the face. It was so hard, it made him black out for a second, and stumble backwards. The object came at him again, this time hitting him in the forehead. He fell over the top of the pool table located outside the bedroom, sprawled on his back, with his arms outstretched in a crucifixion type pose.

He lay on the top of the table, his head bleeding and his eyes quickly swelling up.

"I think you're going to have a black eye or two in the morning," a female voice said.

He could see her standing there, but only make out a shape, not her face. She was holding a flat shovel directly over his head. He was barely conscious, and could feel the pain taking over his senses. The pain was causing him to go into shock. He was getting dizzy, but still he tried to stand using his hands against the table to steady himself. When he grabbed the side of the table, the shovel came down on one hand, and then the other, smashing most of his fingers. He fell backwards again, and lay there looking straight up. He couldn't speak or move and he could barely see. With the darkness of the room, and the fact that both his eyes, and his forehead had just been slammed with a shovel, he was surprised he was even conscious.

He tried to talk, "what do you want?" he muttered.

He noticed a smile on the woman's face come to life. He had seen that smile before, but it had been different than it was now. The smile was a vengeful smile, not a happy one.

"Nothing," she said softly. "Just remember me; always remember the innocence you stole."

When the last word came out of her mouth, the shovel came down hard on his neck, splitting his larynx, and collapsing his esophagus.

The next blow was to his head, and it was the one that did the most damage. The pool table top was slowly turning from green to a dark mixture of red and black. She slowly put the shovel down next to the table, took a rose from her pocket, and placed it between his legs.

He was still. There was no movement at all and, she knew he was dead. The good doctor was deceased, and now he was transporting to whatever afterlife he had made for himself. She found it hard to conceive that he would be seeing any white light or meeting any angels waiting to take him home. She imagined him slipping away into the darkness with the evil shapes she remembered in the movie, *Ghost*. The image of the evil shadows of shapes that would slink up from the depths of hell, and carry the damned person to his resting place, made her smile ironically,

"Good riddance," she whispered.

She turned, and went back into the bedroom where Ben lay in the bed half conscious. He was blubbering in his own spit on the mattress, he wasn't talking, he was only breathing. The drugs she had fed him worked great, he wouldn't wake for some time, maybe just in time for the nice detective to come, and see her work.

She walked up the stairs taking her latex gloves off as she got to the top. She put them in her pocket after she opened the back door. She felt refreshed, and ready for the night to fall on her. She felt as ready as she had ever felt; the vengeance was soothing to her soul, and seeing Ben on the bed, blubbering in his own juice, made her happy. Nearly as happy as seeing Dr. Charles Cranston, bleeding into the pool table felt. She thought about taking Ben out then, but decided he would serve his purpose better where he was.

"Eight ball in the corner pocket," she said to herself, as she shut the door behind her.

Chapter Six

Ryan stood with his partner in the Medical Examiner's office, waiting for the coroner to return from the morgue. They had brought Mr. Williams, to the basement just a few minutes earlier, and had started the autopsy as soon as the office received the body. Ryan was interested in the man, not because of how he was killed, but for the time he was taken out of this world so morbidly.

"Must have been a rotten way to die," Don Breeding commented. "I think you have to wonder whether or not the guy that killed him knew him very well? It doesn't even look like he tried to get out from under the car, does it? It seems like if it was a stranger, he would have gotten out from under the car right away."

Ryan was deep in thought about the morning. He had seen some things others didn't seem to notice in the room, such as the beer bottle. Just like Don, he had noticed it looked as though Mr. Williams didn't try to exit the underside of the car. The other thing he noticed was whoever did this didn't have a great deal of strength. It took several hits on his legs to do the final damage. There had even been more than one hit to his fingers, indicating that the person that did this was either very little or perhaps a woman. He dismissed the thought of it being a child, and focused his mind on the woman end of it. He had noticed that the garage was in really good shape; there was no fight, no sign of a struggle. The culprit in the murder had waited, waited for all the workers to leave for the day, and waited for Mr. Williams, to climb under the car. The person that killed him was obviously very angry with him, but didn't want an altercation. He or she wanted it to be a one-way battle. This didn't seem indicative of a man that could have been on the warpath, or a crime of passion.

"Ryan, did you hear anything I just said?" Don asked.

"I'm sorry," he said as he snapped back out of his thoughts. "Yea, I heard you, and I agree, but I don't think it was a him, I have a hunch it was a woman."

Don sneered in a condescending chuckle, "a woman, why would you think it was a woman?"

The Medical Examiner came into the room before Ryan could answer Don's question, "do you both want to be present for some of the autopsy?" he asked.

The three men walked out, and down the hall. Ryan had been down this hallway many times before, in his short career, and it didn't matter how often he made the walk, he would never get used to it. It seemed that when you were a homicide detective, the city or county morgue could become your second home pretty easily.

It wasn't the death that encircled the walls; it wasn't the fact that sometimes there were dead bodies stacked in the hallway, like lost souls waiting for their fate. It wasn't even that sometimes he knew the people that he came to identify or examine. The thing that bothered him most was the smell, not of the death, but of wasting human life, draining into the walls of solitude, and despair. He felt as if sometimes he could feel the dead looking at him from under the paint and aluminum that carpeted the walls he walked down. He had never made the trip for a death of natural causes, and he longed for that trip, the one time he would come down these hallways for something other than a homicide.

They entered the room where all the autopsies were done. It was huge, with several stainless steel tables arranged in straight lines on both sides. Tonight, both sides were full, toe tags sticking out from under sheets, yellow markers for the dead. Some of the sheets were spotted with blood, and some were as white and smooth, as freshly fallen snow. There was an occasional hand falling restfully from under the sheet, hanging down as if to reach for the floor. He wondered if they covered the dead so they would stay warm. It was always cold in the morgue, cold and full of the smell of death.

Tim William's final resting table was in the middle of one of the rows. His sheet wasn't spotted with blood; it was soaked, so much so, the coroner had wrapped an end around one of his broken and smashed arms, to keep it from dripping on the floor.

The examiner took the sheet at the top, and pulled it down around his chest. His face was badly damaged, and the car had crushed most of the ribs and bones in his chest.

"There won't be much guessing on this one," the examiner said. "I think something crushed this guy," he said in a mocking tone.

Just get on with it Mr. Compassionate," Ryan said. "All we need to know is when he died; we already have the cause figured out."

"Well, by the look of the rigidity, and the temperature of his body, he died sometime last night, probably before nine o'clock."

He took some tweezers out from a tray of tools at the end of the table, and pulled on something that was in the cuts on the victim's knees, "interesting Ryan," he said. "Looks like a fingernail, a woman's fingernail, if I might guess."

The fingernail was long and painted red. It was manicured on one end, and broken with a jagged edge on the other.

"It's fake," the Medical Examiner said, with a bit of surprise in his voice. "Glue on, and a cheap "do it yourself" kind at that. It's not very large either, small, like it would be on a child maybe."

Ryan took the tweezers, and looked at the nail in the light. It was easy to tell it was made of some sort of material that would withstand the abuse of everyday use. The end was perfectly shaped, but the end broken off had a material residue on it.

"It looks like there is something left behind on it," Ryan said to the examiner. "Send the nail over to forensics, and they can get whatever it is off, and perhaps get some DNA out of it."

Just as Ryan was handing the nail back to the examiner, Don received a call on his cell. Ryan was very careful with his phone. He didn't like having everyone flaunting his phone number all over creation. He had read the book by Steven King with the daunting title *"Cell"*, and frankly the devices scared the hell out of him.

Don finished his conversation, and came over to Ryan where he whispered in his ear, "it seems we have another one, Ryan. Some guy just woke up from what he says was forced drug inducement, and says he found a dead guy on his pool table. What's really weird about it is, it's across the street from the one this morning."

Ryan and Don left the morgue, and drove to the address the dispatcher had given them. Ryan was surprised when they parked the car outside the driveway where he had seen the young girl earlier that morning. She had been going inside, and insisted she was just having a little trouble with her father.

When they arrived in the drive, a uniformed officer was standing at the front door. Some of the neighbors had wandered out to see what was happening. There were two ambulances, three police cars, a fire truck, and the county coroner parked either in the street, or in the driveway. To some Ryan was sure it looked as though a serial killer had just inhabited their neighborhood.

"Tell me what we have," Ryan said to the officer at the door.

"As far as we can tell, there is one man dead, and one that says he slept through the whole thing. The coroner is in the basement looking at the body now. My partner has the other man in the living room. He smells like he had one hell of a night, sir."

Ryan and Don went into the house, and looked to the right where an officer was standing over a man that had a blanket around him as he sat in a chair. Another officer was trying to get him to drink some coffee. Ryan told Don they would come back to interview him in a minute. Both headed for the basement to see what had happened.

The room was now lit with very bright halogen lights, positioned in each corner. All of them were pointed directly at a pool table that had a man sprawled out in the middle. The table was soaked with blood, and it was easy to see his face and neck were smashed. Ryan also noticed his hands had been mangled as well. Placed directly between his legs was the red rose, the same shape and size as the one left on Tim Williams, and put exactly in the same location. Next to the table, a flat shovel was leaning, with blood caked on the metal end. It looked almost as if it were placed there so the authorities would find it. One of the CSI's was dusting it for prints. Ryan was sure he probably wouldn't find any, just like the sledgehammer this morning.

Don went over to the side of the table, and bent down close to the body. He put on latex gloves and took out a small plastic zip-lock bag. He reached up to the man's head, and gently pulled a small fragment of something from the wound around what had once been his nose. He held it up, and showed it to Ryan. He placed it in the bag, and stood up once more.

"I think we have a real problem here, Ryan. I think we may have us a serial killer."

Ryan took the bag from Don, and held it at eye level. Inside, Don had placed a small piece of fingernail. It was hardly noticeable that it was painted red, and it was small enough that it was almost not recognizable, but the two men knew what it was, they had seen it earlier.

Ryan looked at the coroner and asked, "any identification on him," as he walked around the table, and opened the door to the room at the far end.

"Yes," he said. "Doctor Charles Cranston, he lives in Sevierville, but practices here in town. I've called his wife, but she's out of town. She's Evelyn Cranston, you know, the Congresswoman."

Both Don and Ryan looked at the coroner with astonishment, "Congresswoman?" Don commented as a question.

"I think we need to talk with the man upstairs," said Ryan. "Thanks Doc, let us know when you get some sort of time of death."

Ryan was thinking about the doctor in the basement, and the fact he had a relatively well-known wife involved in politics. He was anxious to find out if the two victims were connected in any way, or if this was just a random series of events for a disturbed person. He was sure of one thing; the man in the living room didn't kill Dr. Cranston. By the looks of him, he couldn't hardly stand, let alone swing the shovel, which was next to the table.

The two had reached the living room, and with the two officers still present. One was insisting on the man drinking the coffee he had brought from the kitchen.

"Can you excuse us, guys?" Ryan asked. "Don, get Mr.?"

"Hendrickson," the man volunteered.

"Get Mr. Hendrickson a drink, I imagine they're in the refrigerator, Mr. Hendrickson?"

Ben licked his lips, and nodded yes. He longed to slam a beer down right now. He was sick of coffee, and the water the others were trying to force him to drink.

Don left the room, and went to the kitchen. Ryan took a chair from the wall, and turned it around directly in front of Ben. He sat with his legs apart, straddling the chair, "I'm Detective Ryan Rose," he said as he showed his badge. "What's your first name?"

"Ben," he said. "Ben Hendrickson," he told Ryan for the second time.

"Well Ben, can you tell us what happened?"

Don came back into the room carrying three bottles of beer in his hands. He crossed the room, and sat in a chair on the opposite side where Ryan was. He sat the beers on a table, and took out a notebook. He popped the top on one of the beers and put it next to him, and then he opened the second, handing it to Ryan. The third sat unopened on the table. Ben followed him with his eyes the entire time he was walking past, and as he opened the two bottles. When Don took a big swallow; his eyes never left the other beer bottle.

"Let's concentrate, Ben," Ryan told him. "Tell us everything you remember."

"I don't remember much to tell you the truth. I was going upstairs, and I heard something at the back door. I went to investigate, but I had been drinking quite a bit. When I turned around on the stairs, I slipped and fell down them. It took me a couple of minutes to get my bearings, and when I looked up, everything went black. The next thing I knew I was waking up downstairs in the basement. I don't know how I got there, and I don't know how Charles got into the house. He wasn't here when I tried to go upstairs. I got up, and went to the other room and Charles was on the table, dead."

"You knew him?" Don asked.

"Yes, of course. He was my doctor and my friend," he started to cry at that point; "I've known him for years."

"What time did you go upstairs?"

"I don't know what time it was," he paused for a second, "I know it was after ten o'clock last night. I was going up to check on my daughter, you know just look in on her, nothing else, I just wanted to look in on her to make sure she was ok."

Ryan and Don looked at each other. Both thought it was unusual he was so insistent on what he was doing, and why.

"Where's your daughter now?" Don asked.

"I don't know, I haven't seen her since last night. She's probably staying at a friend's house. I have a headache, does anyone have an aspirin?"

Ryan looked at the man, and got a couple of steps closer to him, "I talked to your daughter this morning, Mr. Hendrickson. She was coming home, and told me she was having—father and daughter trouble—is what she called it."

"Why were you here this morning?" Ben asked.

Ryan looked at Don again. Apparently Ben didn't know his neighbor had been killed last night.

"Where were you last night?"

"I got home about six, and I stayed in all night, why?"

"Your neighbor, Mr. Williams, was killed last night in his shop," Don said. "It was a pretty gruesome scene. We were across the street at his house when your daughter walked up to your house. She wasn't in school, and said she was just coming by to get some clothing. Could there be more of a problem than she told my partner?"

"No, there's no problem, just a little disagreement, all of us have them with our teenagers, don't we?"

"Of course," Ryan said as he stood up. "You stay available Mr. Hendrickson," Ryan handed him his business card, "I'm sure we'll have more questions for you."

Ryan and Don got up and walked to the front door, as they did, Ben got up from the chair, walked over to the table, downed the two open beers, and popped open the third. Both men looked at each other, and shook their heads. They knew there was more to this story than he was telling them. It was obvious they weren't going to get it out of him. They would have to find his daughter, and see what she remembered about the night before, and if she had any involvement in this situation.

Chapter Seven

Aubrey and Amy walked out of the school into the cold afternoon. The clouds had formed again, not the kinds you could make shapes out of, but clouds just gray and dreary. They blanketed the sky like a big quilt, holding the cold weather in, and not allowing the warming rays of the sun to break through. Aubrey was sick of the winter, and Amy looked as though she could almost cry when she bundled up to keep the frost out. The two girls walked silently along until they were just off the school grounds.

Amy was the first to break the silence, "what did the principal want?" she asked her friend.

Aubrey stayed silent for quite some time before she answered her friend. The question was straight forward, but Aubrey wasn't sure she could answer Amy the way she needed to be answered. There wasn't a reason not to tell her the truth, but it was hard for her to speak it for some reason.

"Can we talk about it later?" she finally asked.

"Sure, are you still going to stay at my house tonight?" she said nonchalantly.

"Yea," she answered. "I think I need to talk to your mom about this, and when I do, you can sit in and listen, but Amy, I don't want any questions, ok?"

The two girls walked out to the parking lot, and looked for Amy's mother's car to be there. The cold was biting Aubrey. She could hardly stand it. They stood and watched the mist of their breath in the cold.

"I hope your Mom isn't too late," Aubrey said.

"She's usually here by now, but there's a lot of cars in line because of the cold, she'll be along any minute."

The two stood for a few minutes when someone tapped Aubrey on the shoulder. She turned around, and saw the detective that was at her house earlier when she went to get some clothes. Another detective accompanied him this time, one she hadn't seen at the house.

Amy noticed Aubrey looked frightened when she saw the detectives, both of which had their badges in their hands, displayed for both girls to see.

"Miss Hendrickson, can we speak with you for a few minutes?" Ryan asked her.

Aubrey looked as though she wanted to run from the two policemen, but there was really nowhere for her to go. She turned her head both ways, and Amy noticed again that she was extremely nervous.

Amy tried to rescue her friend, "my Mom is supposed to be here any minute, She's picking both of us up."

Don stepped forward in front of Amy, "we're really not looking for a conversation with you, you can go find your mother if you like," he told her.

"Miss Hendrickson, I only have a few questions for you, we can go back inside the school if you like, and we'd be a little warmer in there."

Again, Aubrey looked around as if she wanted to run away, Amy looked just as nervous the more her friend tried to avoid the police. Don stepped forward, and started to take Aubrey's arm and lead her back to the school, when a car drove up along side the four. Amy's Mother got out of the car, looking at the two detectives as if they were intruders.

Ryan took his badge back out and showed it to her, "I'm Detective Ryan Rose, and this is Detective Don Breeding," he offered his hand to Amy's mother.

"Get in the car girls," she said to Amy and Aubrey without shaking Ryan's hand. "Gentlemen, what is the meaning of coming to a school and questioning these girls without their parents?"

"We only have a few questions for Aubrey Hendrickson, are you a relative of hers?" Ryan asked.

"I'm not, but she's staying at our house for a short time, her father needs to be notified that you want to talk with her," she started around to the driver's side of the car; Don stepped in front of her.

"We've just left her father's house, it's the reason we need to talk to her," he said.

"I'm aware of the situation at his house," she said. "He called me, and asked me to notify Aubrey of what happened there last night. The principal of the school met with Aubrey and let her know, so she's aware of everything. Is there anything else you need to tell her?"

Ryan looked at the woman, and wondered why everyone was trying to keep the young girl from them, "we need to ask her some questions about the incident. We can do it here, or she can come down to the station with us. Please ma'am, don't interfere, it's only a few questions."

The woman looked terrified of what was going on, and a small crowd of students was starting to gather, "We're aware of her father's condition, so we can come to your house if you like. You can be present while we ask her what we need, if it would make you more comfortable."

Sara Temple felt as if she was being torn in two, on one hand she felt as if she had to protect Aubrey from whatever it was these men were really after, on the other, she had to think of her own daughter. She wasn't willing to go to jail just to stop them from talking to Aubrey.

Ryan knew the situation was starting to get a little heated, and he wanted to calm everyone down as soon as he could. He could force the girl out of the car, and take her to the station, but with the students around, and the mother almost in a panic, it didn't seem like the thing to do.

Don was faster than Ryan this time, "what's your name ma'am?"

"I don't have to tell you my name," she said.

"I know, I just thought if we knew your name, we could get to a more civilized tone with each other. We're just trying to do our job, nothing more. It's cold, and I for one want to go home and get a hot cup of coffee."

The comment seemed to calm her down a little, and Ryan agreed, it was cold, and it would be better in a house or the school.

"My name is Sara Temple," she told them.

"Well, Mrs. Temple, we can follow you to your house, or we can even go down to the coffee shop if you like, you tell us what you want."

The crowd continued to form, and now the principal, along with another teacher, came out of the school. Ryan and Don immediately brought out their badges again, showing them to the two men. Ryan told the principal what was going on, and he told the two he was aware of what went on at the house that afternoon. He turned to Mrs. Temple, and urged her to let Aubrey come into the school to talk with the detectives. He also assured her he would be responsible for her, and would make sure she got home immediately after the detectives were finished.

Aubrey got out of the car, and went back in the school with the men. Her face showed the worry she had felt earlier with Amy. She didn't know why they wanted to talk to her, she wasn't even home when everything happened, but they obviously felt a need to question her.

When they got back in the school, the heat in the hallway did make her feel better. Students and teachers alike were waiting along the hall on the way to the school office. Everything that happened outside had increased the curiosity of everyone within earshot of what was going on. High school was always good at doing that sort of thing. Sometimes, it took only seconds to spread a happening to everyone.

Once inside the office, Aubrey sat in a chair against the wall. The principal took his seat behind his desk, with Ryan and Don remaining on their feet. Ryan went over to Aubrey, and tried to speak in a quiet, calm voice.

"I saw you this morning at your house, right?" he asked her.

"Yes," she replied.

"You said you and your father were having some sort of trouble and you were just going to get some clothes, correct?"

"Yes," she said again.

"Was there anyone else in the house while you were there?"

"Not that I know of, only my father."

"Where was he?"

"He was in the upstairs bathroom, he looked drunk. It looked like he wanted to take a bath, and left the water running until it was all over the floor. I turned it off, made sure he wouldn't slip into the water, got my clothes and left."

"Are you sure he was in the bathroom when you left the house?"

What the girl was saying seemed to be the same as her father had told them just a little while ago. Neither seemed to know how, nor why he went to the basement, and she wasn't mentioning anything about the doctor, about knowing him, or why he was in the house.

"Did you know the man killed in the house," Don asked.

Ryan thought the question was a bit harsh to ask the girl, and when he finished, her facial expression changed from sadness to horror. She went white, then sat back in her chair with a gasp of air. Her arms went limp to her sides, and she stared into the room as if nothing, and no one was in there with her. It seemed as if she went completely blank from the world.

Ryan stood up, somewhat shocked by her immediate change in appearance, "are you ok, Miss Hendrickson?" he asked her.

"I think I need to take her to my house now," Sara said to the two detectives. "She looks as though she is going to pass out," she turned to the principal and asked, "is the school nurse still here?"

"I'm all right Mrs. Temple," she said putting her hand on Sara's waist. "I did know him; he was our doctor for a long time. It's a shock to think of him dead, and even a bigger shock how he died."

"Why do you think he was in your house in the middle of the day?" Ryan asked her.

"I don't know, maybe my dad called him to come over."

"Your father said he wasn't aware of Doctor Cranston being there."

Aubrey shrugged her shoulders, and looked as though she knew nothing about Dr. Cranston's motive for being at her house.

"I think we have enough for right now, but please let us know if you're going back to your house. Your father has checked into a hotel for the time being until we can get things cleaned up at the house."

Aubrey and Sara got up to leave. Amy was waiting in the outer office for them, and Ryan looked through the window, watching her stand.

"Just one more thing," Ryan said to the two women. "Can I see your hands, Aubrey?"

Aubrey had been wearing gloves for the entire time they were questioning her. The gloves were multi colored, and looked extremely warm. Aubrey hesitated when asked to take them off; she was still cold from standing outside for so long, "please, may I see your hands?" Ryan asked once more.

She took both gloves off, and offered her hands to the detective. She held them out with her palms pointed up, so Ryan reached out, and turned them over so he could see the nails and the top of her fingers. Both detectives reacted at the same time with a quiet gasp of surprise. Each nail on her hands was perfect, and each nail was painted a different color, including red.

"Thank you," was all that Ryan could muster in response.

The ladies left the room, and Ryan sat down in front of the principal's desk. Don found a chair at the back of the room, and noted something in his small book.

"Can we ask you a few questions?" he asked the principal

Ryan had always wondered if people that used a desk all the time, became used to the fixture to sort of help them with feeling a little less significant, or more powerful. He had seen many people take advantage of a desk this way. Instead of taking the time to sit and talk to your face, they used the desk as prop, to help redeem their sense of worth. Ryan was positive this man was using the desk to help him bolster his ability to read the two detectives, and what they wanted from him. He had watched him as they questioned the girl, and noticed he really didn't change any of his expressions. It was like he either didn't hear what was being said, or he already knew the answers. He seemed distracted and unattached to the rest of the people in the room.

He moved two pencils from the center of the desk, and put them in a small cup that had writing on the side, "World's Best Teacher", printed in gold.

"Of course," he said, looking back up at Ryan.

"What kind of student is Aubrey?"

"One of the best in school, as far as scholastics are concerned; she doesn't seem to have the best social skills, but her studies are second to none. She is an excellent speaker in front of the other students, but when asked by any of us to speak, well, it's almost as if her mind shuts off, and she can't think of a thing to say."

"Do you know anything about her home life or her father and mother?"

"We know that her mother left about three years ago, just up and walked out on her and her father. We offered her counseling at the time, but her father wouldn't let her attend any of it. When I tried to talk with him on the phone about it, he just hung up on me."

"Does he attend any of the functions here?"

He thought for a moment, "no, he really doesn't, we've tried to schedule talks with him, more to tell him how intelligent his daughter is than anything, and help him achieve some scholarship money for her college. He never returns any notes, or calls us. After several attempts, we kind of gave up on him, and just told Aubrey how to go about the application process."

"Didn't you think that was a little strange, I mean don't most parents revel in the knowledge that their kid is that smart?" Don asked from the other side of the room.

"Not really, detective, we have several parents that don't participate in anything at the school. It's a shame, but in this day and age, we have become the majority stockholder in some of these kids' future. Parents have become so immersed in their daily lives; they have forgotten that they have a part in the bringing up of a teenager."

"Has she ever tried to open up to any teacher or counselor?" Ryan asked.

"About a year ago, she came into the office after a visit to the school nurse. The nurse had told her she could go home for the day, because she wasn't feeling well. After the visit she came to the office, and asked if she could just stay here until school was out, she really didn't want to go to her house. We asked if her father was home, and she told us he was, but she didn't want to go home yet, she just wanted to stay in the office and read a book. We all thought it was a bit odd, but let her remain here until school was out. She read for a while, and then went to the nurse's office, and took a nap. It was like she was afraid to go home."

"Did you ask her why?"

"Of course, but she was reluctant to talk to me, or the assistant principal. She did open up a little bit to the nurse, but nothing specific in terms of a problem at home, she only said her father had started drinking, and she didn't want to see it that day. Sad, if you ask me. You have a daughter that bright, and you ignore her and her potential. Since then, we kind of watch her a little closer than some of our other students, but we've never seen any reason to suspect any abuse on anyone's part."

"Thanks for your time," Ryan stood up, and offered his hand to the principal. "We may be in touch again, I'm sorry for the trouble outside today, next time we'll come in and get you first."

"One other thing detectives, she is extremely close to Amy, the two are inseparable it seems. We think sometimes it's almost an unhealthy attraction on Amy's part."

Don and Ryan left the office with another thank you to the principal, with neither saying anything, until they got back into their car. Both were deep in thought about the things that had happened during the day. Some things were somewhat bizarre, and it had certainly been a day of surprises. It was, after all, very unusual to have two murders with similar circumstances. Then to have the two victims living that close together kept both men's minds wondering about the connection.

Ryan started back to the station to report to their Captain on the day's happenings. They drove in silence for a long time. Don finally broke the deadlock of silence.

"Do you think this young girl is capable of doing this?" he asked Ryan.

Ryan almost stopped the car in the middle of the street, but maintained control. They were partners, and partners sometimes thought, and acted alike after years of being with each other. It was a little unusual for short time partners to be this in tune with each other.

Ryan couldn't help but be amazed at how much the two of them thought alike, when it came to cases like these.

"I was just thinking that myself," he said. "Do I think she's capable, I don't know, but I know she sure seems nervous about all of this. Did it seem that way to you?"

Don only nodded at the question. He did feel the tension when they interviewed the young girl. He also got the feeling the principal wasn't giving them all the facts, or maybe he was just trying to protect her. Don had honed his feelings about people, and if you could get Ryan to admit it, he was usually right about most of them. This guy, he thought, wasn't' telling them everything.

Ryan broke up his train of thought, "I think we need to go see the Medical Examiner again," he said.

He immediately turned the car back towards the morgue they had visited earlier in the day. Ryan thought maybe the examiner may have picked up what the substance was on the first victim, and maybe they found the same stuff on the good doctor.

When they got inside the morgue, they went directly to the Medical Examiner's office. He was just sitting down at his desk, with a well-deserved cup of coffee.

"Have you finished the autopsy on Dr. Cranston?" Ryan asked.

"No, we aren't doing an autopsy on him Ryan, seems his wife has made other arrangements. They just left with his body heading for the crematorium. He's going to be cremated tomorrow morning."

"There's a murder investigation ongoing here, Sol, what do you mean he's been picked up already? SOP is an autopsy!"

I guess when you have people like your wife in high places, you can put a little pressure on our bosses and things get, shall we say, overlooked."

"Bullshit, we need to find some things out before they destroy evidence we may need."

"If you're talking about the substance we found on the first victim, you're in luck, I found the same substance on him. I got it off before they came and got him."

"Has the lab gotten back with you on the first victim?"

"Yea, seems our fingernail had some latex on it, probably from a latex glove. I think the second victim has the same substance on him, but we'll know more tomorrow."

"You get with me as soon as you find out, I want to know as soon as you do, ok?"

"You're the boss Ryan," he said in a matter of fact tone.

"By the way, good job, thanks for your help," Ryan patted him on the back as they walked out.

"Why would his wife want this shoved under the rug so quick?" Ryan asked Don as they went outside. "It seems to me she would be the one trying to get to the bottom of her husband's murder."

"Maybe we should make a trip to her house, but we better tread carefully, you know how they get when we start talking to politicians," he pretended to shudder with fear at the comment.

"You're right," said Ryan. "We'll put her on our list for first thing in the morning, maybe she can shed some light on this dark mess. In the meantime, it's been an eventful day, what do you say to a beer before we call it a night?"

"Now you're talking my language, let's roll."

Chapter Eight

Amy sat in her bedroom watching Aubrey sleep on the floor. Her thoughts were about the day's happenings, and how she could help her friend handle all the pressure that was suddenly placed on her. She relished in the fact Aubrey had chosen to stay with her for a few days. Her friendship meant everything to Amy, but she didn't think Aubrey knew just how much. She would do anything to keep her safe, and help her.

Aubrey had done so much for Amy; her ability to teach was as evident as her ability to learn. Amy had a learning disability, and Aubrey had helped her through some very hard times in high school. She was very unpopular in all of her classes, because she couldn't understand half of what was taught to her. The kids were relentless in their constant harassment. They called her stupid, and dummy, and sometimes would talk and act like she was "retarded", as they called it. School was extremely difficult for her, and Aubrey soon made that awkward time bearable.

Aubrey had changed everything with one simple hello in the lunchroom on a particularly bad day Amy was having. Her caring nature brought her to Amy, and Amy was determined to help her out of all of this, even if she didn't know what all of it was.

For now, Aubrey slept, with her breathing deep, and rhythmic. She had one arm under her pillow while she lay on her side. The covers were half on, and half off, and Amy enjoyed watching her sleep so innocently. Amy watched for a few more minutes, and then began to lay herself down to bed when Aubrey suddenly said something. Amy wasn't sure if she had heard right, so she hiked herself back up on her elbow, and listened. After a few minutes, she didn't hear anything else, and lay back down to venture into dreamland. She was at the point between consciousness and sleep, a point where you are still aware of the surroundings you are in, but slip into something you may think is real, but isn't. Her eyes were closed, but her ears were still alive to the sounds of night in a house where everyone is quiet.

She heard the noise once, and dismissed it as something houses do to keep you guessing. When her father was alive he used to call it "settling", but Amy never really understood that term. The second knock was much louder, and Amy jolted to reality with a jerk. The same time Amy came to life; Aubrey sat up on the floor and rubbed her eyes.

"What was that?" she asked Amy.

The room was still dark, so Amy switched on the small lamp next to her bed. The knock came again, a steady banging at the front door. Both girls realized the noise they heard was someone trying to get their attention. They got up simultaneously from their sleeping spots.

"It's ok," Amy's mother called from the hallway, "you girls stay there, I'll get it," she said sleepily.

They heard her go to the door, and could hear the mumbling of a man speaking with Mrs. Temple. Amy felt fear in her stomach. They never got visitors this late at night. She looked at Aubrey, and could see the fear had also encased her. The two girls sat silent as Amy's mother talked to the man for what seemed like hours. She raised her voice only once to the man, sending him on his way with the door shut in his face.

The two girls watched as she leaned up against the front door with her hands still clasping the doorknob. She had a look of total despair, staring blindly into space. She finally realized that the two girls were standing, watching her, both chewing their nails nervously.

"I didn't know you were there," she finally said. "You can both go back to bed now."

"Mom," Amy said. "Who was that at the door, I mean c'mon you can't expect us to just ignore that, can you?"

Sara looked at the floor, shaking her head, "of course not, I'm sorry. Both of you come into the living room, and we can talk."

All three headed for the living room, Aubrey had that uneasy feeling in the pit of her stomach. She was thinking about what Amy's mother was about to say to them. She felt like she knew already what the problem at the door was, but she was reluctant to even guess that she was right. She knew the voice, she had heard it many times at her house, but she didn't dare let on to them that she recognized who he was. She merely sat in a chair, and waited for Mrs. Temple to spill the beans to Amy. It was evident from the look on her face that she knew what was going on now.

"Aubrey," she started, staring directly at her. "The man at the door was, well let's say, he was very, very drunk. If my doorframe had not have held him up, he probably would have fallen right there on the sidewalk. He told me his name was Bobby Minor, and he was a friend of your father's. He insisted on coming in to see you, and when I asked him why, he told me that you would know why."

"How did he know I was here?" she asked, starting to cry.

Aubrey's secret, the secret that she tried so hard to hide from everyone, was getting ready to come out of the darkness she chose to keep it in. She was having trouble controlling her emotions and she knew once Mrs. Temple said it she would break down.

"I'm getting to that, honey," Mrs. Temple continued. "I told him that he couldn't come into my house, that you were sleeping, and he needed to go back to where he came from. He told me he was your boyfriend, but I knew better, Aubrey. He was too old, and looked as though he was sneaking around to find you, so I asked him the same question that you asked me, and he told me your father told him you were here."

She stopped for a minute to gather her composure, "he told me that he was here to take you away from all this, and he loved you. He said you were going to be with him for the rest of your life. It took me a minute to convince him that you were not the one he was talking about, that he was mistaken, drunk and didn't know where he was. I told him if he didn't leave that I was going to call the police, and have him arrested."

Aubrey was now in a full tilt cry, her sobbing was becoming uncontrollable. She sat with her head in her hands, alone as she had ever been. She hadn't felt this alone since her mother left that night.

Amy came over and sat next to her, put her arm around her, and held her tight while she sobbed. Amy's mother just stood there wondering what part of this mystery would unfold next.

Aubrey tried to stop crying, "it's not what you think, Mrs. Temple," she said. "I do know who he is, but he's not my boyfriend, he's not even a friend. He's a friend of my father's, and he comes to our house every once in a while to drink and—"

She hesitated, because she wasn't sure that she could say the words that would explain the situation. She had never spoken of this out loud to anyone. She wished that her mother were there to help her through the toughest night of her life.

"He comes, and my father allows him to come upstairs, and get in bed with me."

She could hardly believe that she said it to them. She opened her eyes, and looked at her two friends. Amy was staring at her in disbelief, with both having the look of someone that had been stunned beyond anything that they could expect. Aubrey got the sick feeling in her belly again. Amy's mother looked at her, with what Aubrey perceived as contempt. She glared at her as if she already knew what was happening to her, as if the guilt was suddenly written on her face.

Amy got up from beside her, and went to stand next to her mother. She was starting to cry, and it became evident that it was her, that needed the shoulder now. She buried her head in her Mother's shoulder and cried loudly.

Aubrey got up from her chair, watching the two women, both crying, as Aubrey stood alone on one side of the room. She started to tell them that it wasn't her fault, but decided that they probably wouldn't believe her. It was just like her mother, and father. Their breakup was because of her, now the only friends she had, hated her too. She walked to the front door, and opened it.

Amy looked out from her mother, "Aubrey, stop, you don't have to go," she said. "I'm sorry, it was just a shock, we had no idea that you, that you…"

Amy wasn't sure what she meant to say to her. She wasn't crying because of what she did, she was crying because of what happened to her best friend.

Aubrey's embarrassment was too much to bear. She had told her friend what had happened, and she too had turned against her. She stood at the door for a few seconds more, and then rushed out, running down the street. She had finally had enough. It was time to confront her father.

Amy ran to the door, and snatched it open. She went out in the front, and looked down the street only to see Aubrey running away. She felt terrible; both her, and her mother had acted horribly to her. She turned, and went inside. She had to convince her mother they needed to go after her, calm her down, and find out the entire situation.

Chapter Nine

Bobby Minor staggered back to his apartment downtown. He had driven his car, knowing he shouldn't, and that another DUI would probably put him behind bars for good. Still, he felt as if he had to get to Aubrey. He had heard about the murders on the news, and had found her father at the hotel after Ben had called him. The two had gotten drunk, and Ben told him where Aubrey had decided to stay during this tough time. Ben passed out in his chair, and Bobby managed the guts to go over to the house convince Aubrey to come with him.

If she would have him, he would quit drinking and doing the occasional drugs, straighten out his life, and settle down with her. Ben hadn't told him she was at that bitch's house. He thought she was alone at some house the police had provided. He was prepared to fight for her, but in his current condition, there would be no fight. He couldn't even manage to form the words he needed to explain the relationship he had with Aubrey. Tomorrow would be another day for that explanation.

He opened the door to his apartment on the second floor. The lights were all out except a small radio on the nightstand in the corner. The red numbers illuminated the time with 3:10 showing brightly in the darkness. He fumbled for the light switch, but after several tries, he gave up, and just threw his keys where he thought the table would be located next to the window.

He had lived in this hole for three years already, not really looking for a nicer place to reside. A three-room apartment was plenty big for him. His kitchen was filthy, with dishes piled in the sink, and food caked on the stove he very seldom used anymore. To say he was a slob was probably an understatement. He vowed in his head to do better starting tomorrow. Of course he had promised himself that before plenty of times.

He staggered to the kitchen, and made the light the very first time. Feeling a sense of pride, he went to the refrigerator, and got himself a beer to celebrate. He didn't have to work the next day, so a grand drunk was certainly in order for the night, of course it had already been more than he bargained for. He went back into the other room, and sat down in front of his TV. He switched it on, and the channel he had watched last had an infomercial going. This time of the morning always had these types of advertisements on, and Bobby hated them all. He switched the channel, and another was on, something about weight loss. Bullshit, he thought to himself, and changed the channel one more time.

After changing channels until there were no more to check, he put the remote down, and thought about Aubrey and her father for a minute. If her father told him where she was, surely he wanted him to be with her. He must think he could take care of her. He decided he would go to Ben's hotel, and see if Ben could talk some sense into Aubrey for him.

The night was cold, bitterly cold to be exact. He had put on a coat, but only had some light clothing under it. The coat didn't help much against the winter weather. The snow was still heavy, for the most part, but some had melted during the day, and the remnants of it created ice patches all over the parking lot. There were cars parked in every direction imaginable in the apartments, including one parked directly behind his. He had managed a pretty straight line in the shot to his spot. Others that had come after him had made attempts, but it looked as though they had missed. At least most of them did. He looked around, and saw no one in the lot, so he wasn't sure which apartment belonged to the wayward car.

"I'll have to walk," he said out loud. "Shit, it's cold."

He had a beer in one hand, and his remaining six or seven from a twelve pack under his other arm. The beer would come in handy for Ben. It seemed he always needed just a little encouragement to get him going.

The hotel that the police had put Ben in was just a couple of blocks from where Bobby was. He found walking hard, between the staggering and the ice, he was having quite a time navigating the sidewalks, and his attempts to stay on them sometimes went a little wayward. He trudged on, not making the best of time along the way, but steadily going in the right direction.

He was a small man, and sometimes he was mistaken for a kid when it was dark enough. He wore a blue jacket and jeans, with boots that were well worn from working in them constantly. Several times in his life he was asked for his ID when he went to liquor stores, but other times his youthful looks came in handy. He admitted, as he got older he was showing some bulge around the middle, but for the most part he was in fair shape. He could walk miles, if he had to, and walking this night was easy, except for the occasional misstep. He whistled lightly a tune that was unrecognizable, and had forgotten completely about his confrontation with the lady earlier in the evening.

When he turned the corner, he found himself getting closer to the hotel where Ben was. He could see the light from the sign ahead, and suddenly wondered if Ben would still be awake. Ben was notorious for falling asleep, or passing out in front of the television. Bobby thought a knock on the door would get him up though. Anticipation got him walking a little faster, and straighter. He was concentrating on his trip and suddenly he heard a noise behind him.

He turned around, almost falling when he did so, and looked to see if someone was there. He saw no one.

"Probably a cat," he mumbled, and turned back around.

He walked a few more steps, and heard a louder noise, closer this time. He tried to spin around this time, and slipped, crashing to the ground in a clump. The beer he was holding stayed in his hand, but the others went flying to the ground, and leaving a loud breaking sound as the liquid poured onto the ground.

Even through the numbness of drunkenness he felt the pain in his leg. He grabbed at the bottom part of it, and felt the bone protruding out of his pants. The shock kept him from screaming as he squirmed on the ground holding the broken part of his lower leg together. He tried desperately to regain control, but the cold ground, and the pain were immense. He felt the urge to pee coming as he let his bladder go, which made things warmer, but only for a minute. The cold was getting to him quickly, and he was amazed at how fast he sobered up on the ground. He could smell the mixture of the beer that had spilled and the urine he had just let soak through his jeans.

He tried to let go of his leg, but felt it start to bend into an unrecognizable angle, so he grabbed it with both hands and held on tight. He winced with pain, and decided screaming for help would be the next move. He was getting up the strength to yell when he heard the noise one more time. It was loud, and sounded as if it was right behind him. He tried to turn, but the angle he was laying on the ground prevented him from getting all the way around. All he could see were two legs, standing close, but not close enough for him to touch.

"I'm glad you're here," he said in a whisper. "Please help me, I broke my leg, I need someone to help me to the hospital."

There was no answer from the shadow he saw standing over him, he tried again, "c'mon dammit, I need help, now!

The shadow still showed no response to his cries, only silence from above his head. Slowly he turned the other way, trying to get a better vantage of who was standing over him. All he could see were two legs, and the shadow of the person. He started to cry.

"Please, help me, my leg is broken, I'm in horrible pain, please get me some help."

"I'll help you," a woman's voice said in a matter of fact tone. "I'll help you if you remember me."

The ice pick came hard down on his hands holding his leg together. The pain shot through his arms as he shot backwards, trying to let go of the wounded leg. His head went back, and hit the sidewalk, taking all of his vision away. He could see stars, and his first impulse was to grab the back of his head, but his hands were firmly stuck to his leg, with the pick buried into the muscle. He screamed, loud, as loud as he could, but he couldn't hear it. Others in the neighborhood could though.

The next blow hit him in the middle of his forehead between his eyes. The pick went deep into his brain, and there were no more screams, no more memories, only silence as she stood over him, surveying the death stare he had on his face.

"Now can you see me?" she asked. "Now do you know who I am?"

She turned, and walked away from his body, lying on the sidewalk, no longer worrying about his broken leg, or how he would get out of the cold. He was still, deadly still, one final wisp of breath drifted from his lips, and faded into the cold weather as the air escaped from his lungs for the final time. His stare was vacant, and his whole body was limp with both hands still holding on to his leg. His leg had fallen to a ninety-degree angle as his hands lost their grip with one of the ice picks sticking out.

It had happened fast, maybe too fast for her liking, he had never even seen her face. He went to hell not knowing who it was that put him there. She didn't feel any satisfaction with this one, not like the two before. Both of them had seen who she was, and the look on their faces when they recognized her was worth everything she knew she would eventually get. She simply turned away from him, and walked away.

Ben Hendrickson was sitting in front of the television when he heard the screams from outside the hotel. They sounded as if they were close, close enough to make out, but if the TV wasn't in between commercial and program, he probably wouldn't have heard it. He got up, and looked out the front window. He saw a shadow move from in front of his door.

He snapped back into the room, frightened to open the curtain again. He slowly stepped back to the window, pulled the curtain back, and tried to get his eyes adjusted to the semi light of the outside. This time he saw nothing at his door, this time he saw the face clearly, standing directly in front of the window looking in. It was Aubrey, standing there with tears in her eyes.

"Open the door, Daddy," she said. "I want to talk to you."

Ben Hendrickson stood by the front door taking a minute to gather his thoughts. The last meeting with his daughter had been one he really wanted to forget. He had lost his ability to resist her great looks, and amazing personality. He had always tried to quit taking advantage of her with his friends, but the booze, and guilt had taken its toll with him. He couldn't anymore quit that, than quit drinking. The only thing that kept him sane was he always got drunk before he offered up his daughter's body to the men that wanted her.

He opened the door slowly, and Aubrey stood before him shivering in the cold outside. She had a look on her face that showed how concerned she was, and how much she dreaded the meeting with her father.

"Come in," he told her. "You must be freezing."

She came in the door, and immediately smelled the nauseating fragrance of beer and sweat. She could see the trash can full of beer bottles, and already the room was a mess. Dirty clothes, and trash were thrown everywhere, and both beds in the room were messed up. She couldn't believe someone could do this to a room in just a few short hours of living there. She walked over to a chair by the window, and took the clothes that were thrown there, and put them on the bed.

"Daddy, tonight someone came to Mrs. Temples' house, and tried to get me to go with him. It was Bobby Minor, do you remember him?"

"Yea," he said with his head down. "He was here earlier; we kind of got drunk together."

"Did you tell him where I was?"

Ben couldn't answer, which gave Aubrey the answer she was looking for. He would often avoid the question with silence, indicating he knew what she was talking about.

"I had to tell Mrs. Temple about you, and your friends," she said. "I embarrassed myself beyond belief because you can't quit blaming me for Mom leaving. Now I don't know if I have a place to stay, if I have a place to live, or if my life will even be here tomorrow."

Ben just sat in front of his daughter with his head down. He did feel sorry; he said to himself it wouldn't happen again. He never opened his mouth to tell his daughter he was guilty of all the things she was accusing him of.

"What happened today in the house, how did Doctor Cranston get inside, and who would have killed him like that?"

He looked up for the first time since she came in. If the truth were known, he thought Aubrey was the one that came in and killed him. He wouldn't have blamed her either; Doctor Cranston was one of the worst of the men he had allowed up to her room.

"I don't know the last thing I remember I was upstairs, and then I woke up in the basement with him on the pool table, dead. The police asked me the same question, and I still can't answer it."

He looked over at the small fridge on the other side of the room. He wanted to get up, and get the beer that sat waiting inside. He licked his lips, and at the same time looked at the clock on the nightstand. It read 4:25. He suddenly felt extremely tired, so tired that he needed to go to bed, now, he thought.

"Here's the deal, you no longer control my life, I will find my own way, and you will stop sending those perverted drunk son-of-a-bitches to me. I will turn you in and all of them if I hear one more time from any of them, which includes Bobby Minor. I think that's as clear as I can make it."

She felt the tears starting to come, and she didn't want to cry in front of him. It was the most important thing right now to show strength, even if she didn't believe it herself. She got up to leave the room. She needed to go back to Amy's house, and try to explain what had gone on that night.

"You mean you won't ever see me again?" he asked her. "I really don't want that Aubrey, I know I've been terrible to you, but I need you, I need you to be my daughter," he started to cry openly to her.

"You should have thought of that before you turned me into a whore," she slammed the door behind her, and started walking back to Amy's.

When she rounded the front of the hotel, she noticed the police cars at the end of the street. There had to be twenty of them along with an ambulance, and a fire truck. She had heard sirens when she walked up to the hotel, but didn't pay attention to them. You frequently heard the shrill sound of sirens in the city. She watched for a few seconds, and decided she really didn't need to see what was going on. She turned, and walked away from the excitement at the other end of the street.

She walked along the street, bundled up from the cold, hoping no one would come along, and cause trouble for her. She was just thinking that it was nice that you could still walk in Knoxville late at night, and not have to worry about crime. A car passed her, and came to an abrupt stop. The tires chirping to a stop scared her, and made her automatically jump to the side up against a building. She turned, and saw two men getting out of the car, both wearing what appeared to be suits.

"Aubrey," one called to her. "It's me, Detective Rose, and you need to stay right where you are."

Both Ryan, and Don, got out of the car. Don with his gun at the ready, but he held it tight to his side. They walked over to Aubrey, and stood in front of her.

Ryan looked into her eyes but spoke to Detective Breeding, "it's seems that for the last couple of days every time we find a dead body, this young lady seems to be around, does it seem strange to you?"

Chapter Ten

Amy and her mother came around the corner, and saw the police cars and the ambulance blocking the street. Police barriers prevented them from continuing on their way, and a uniformed officer stood in front of Sara's car, trying to direct them to an alternate route. She stopped the car, and rolled down the window. When she did, he came over, and started to tell her she needed to move on.

"Can I ask what happened here?" She interrupted him before he could finish. "We're looking for someone, a young girl, this isn't her is it?"

"No ma'am," he said in a thick southern accent. "This is something else, you'll have to move along now," he finished, tipping the end of his cap.

There was a sigh of relief in the car from both women, although it seemed as if the officer was being a bit evasive in his answer. Amy looked around, noticing the sheet covering a body on the sidewalk not far from where they were. There were dark stains on the sheet that made her quickly turn away. She also noticed that not far up the street were two men standing with what appeared to be a young woman. She could only see shadows from her vantage point, but could tell there was a car in the street, and the two men were talking to another person. The two men had the other person pinned against the wall in an intimidating stance. Amy asked her mom to drive around the block to see if they could get closer, she had a feeling it was Aubrey, at the other end the men's conversation.

Amy felt as if she had let her friend down back at the house, and even though her mother didn't say so, she had a feeling she had the same guilt. Her mother agreed to drive around the block, but told Amy if another policeman asked them to leave, she would have no choice. They pulled up on the other side of the car where the two men were talking. The police barrier wasn't up on this end, so they were right along side of the car the two men were driving. When they drove up, one of the men came directly to the car.

Sara rolled her window down again, "is that Aubrey Hendrickson?" she asked him as he walked up.

"Mrs. Temple," Detective Breeding greeted her. "What are you two ladies doing here at this hour?"

"We're looking for Aubrey," Amy said. "Is that her?"

Amy's mother put her finger to her lips to indicate to Amy not to ask any more questions. If the two detectives had found Aubrey, out at this hour, and were questioning her on the spot, Sara knew they must suspect her of whatever had happened up the street.

"Aubrey is going with us, if you want, call the station in the morning, and we'll tell you whether or not she can leave with you."

Reluctantly, Amy, and her mother drove away slowly. Don walked back over to where his partner had Aubrey. She was standing with her back to the wall, and Ryan was in front of her.

"What are you doing out so early?" Ryan asked.

"I came down to see my father," she quickly responded. "We had some things we needed to get out in the open, and I didn't think it should wait.

"What time did you get there?" Ryan asked her.

"I don't know, I walked from Amy's house down here, I was there only a few minutes, and left."

Ryan looked at Don, and then looked back to Aubrey, "let's go to the hotel, and see what he has to say about all of this. Hopefully he's going to be sober enough to talk to you."

"He's not," Aubrey said. "He was drunk, and we fought, I had to get something off my chest, what's this all about anyway?"

Both Don, and Ryan, was surprised at the question. They hadn't told her Bobby Minor was sprawled out on the sidewalk less than a block away. They had both assumed she knew why all the police cars were there.

"Aubrey looked stunned for a minute, "that's not my father up there, is it?" she asked looking up at the circumstances being played out.

"No, that's not your father," Ryan told her.

"Who is it then?" she asked.

"I think we all need to go down to the station, and see what you know about all of this. The cold doesn't help anything, and we've got more questions for you."

They took Aubrey's arm, and started walking back to the car. Ryan had thought earlier in the day that she was probably involved in the two killings. Now a third person was dead, and she was in the area again. The chief would be very interested in what she had to say, so Ryan and Don felt they had no choice but to take her in.

"Am I under arrest?" she asked both of them.

"Not yet," Don told her. "We just want to ask you about the days turn of events, and why you're down here along with another dead man. First we're going to the hotel to see if your father is ok."

They put her in the car, and started down to the hotel. The coroner had arrived, and was putting the body in the car as they drove into the parking lot of the hotel. The ambulance had left, and some of the excitement was over for the small number of people gathered on the street.

It always amazed Ryan that no matter what time something happened, there was always an audience looking for the one thing the neighbor may not know. In this case there were four or five couples from the hotel, and a few single people standing around watching. Ryan noticed one of the observers looked especially well dressed for the time of the morning. She stood out even more because of where they were in the city.

They turned into the hotel lot, and got out to go to the room where Ben was staying. Ryan expected to find him passed out on the chair in the room. They had bought him plenty of beer earlier when they dropped him off. Ryan thought if he were in his own element, maybe he would remain quiet, and unable to start any trouble.

Aubrey sat in the back of the car, looking as though she had lost her best friend. Ryan wasn't sure what she had been through, but he was convinced the whole story would play out eventually. He was cautious that she was involved in all of the murders that had happened over the past hours. Don on the other hand was convinced she was the one with something to hide, and if she wasn't the murderer, she knew who was.

A knock on the door revealed nothing at first. There wasn't any answer. Ryan tried to look through the window, but the curtain was closed enough that he couldn't see in the room. He knocked again, and got the same result, he turned to Don.

"Go to the desk, and see if they have a master key for this room," he told him.

When Don walked away, Ryan went back to the car, and opened the door, "was your father ok when you left?" he asked her.

"I told you, we talked for a couple of minutes, and I left. He was upset, but he was ok. You still didn't tell me who that was up the street," she said.

"Listen," he knelt down next to her to see if he could reassure her. "The man up the street is dead, and that's the third death you've been around. We need to know what you were doing down here, and what your connection to all of these murders is."

Aubrey only stared at Ryan with a blank look on her face, "I told you, I was here to see my father," she turned, and looked straight ahead, ignoring Ryan, tears running down her cheeks.

Don came back with the manager of the hotel. He was dressed only in sweat pants, and a dirty tank top. Don shrugged his shoulders when they passed Ryan, knowing his partner would be thinking of how cold it was to be dressed like that.

"You guys better have a good reason for waking me up this early," he said as he went passed.

Ryan thought to himself that the man was just being grumpy this early, and besides, what would he do to them if they didn't have a good reason.

"Just open the door," Don told him.

The man grumbled something none of them could hear, or understand, and slipped the key into the slot. The door opened, and all three moved back in shock at the sight in the room.

Don was the first to speak, "damn Ryan, look at this, what the hell happened in here?"

Directly in front of them the wall was covered in large blotches of what appeared to be blood. Both beds in the room were unmade, and one was covered in the same red substance, the bedspread was soaked with blood. Both walls were streaked in different areas with fingerprints, and handprints that went from the middle of the wall to the floor. The television was on the floor with glass broken out of the tube, and the chairs were both turned over next to the bed. The table that sat in the corner was broken into several pieces.

Ryan pulled out his gun, and slowly went into the room. He went to the bathroom, and slapped the door open. The floor of the room had the blood thick in areas, and the mirror was almost completely covered with bright red streaks. He looked in the shower, but there was no one in the room. He put his gun back in his holster, and turned back to the manager.

"Are people in the rooms next to this one?" he asked.

He shook his head no, "the only other people in the hotel are upstairs," he said.

"Don, get on the radio, and tell the station to send forensics down here. Ryan was stepping carefully around the room, looking under the beds, and searching in the closets to see if there was any indication of a body.

"Looks like she got plenty off her chest," Don said in a sarcastic tone.

"There's no on in here, it's empty," Ryan worked his way back to the door, and outside.

Aubrey sat in the back of the car looking at the hotel room. She noticed the manager as he opened the door and saw he was outwardly upset. Detective Rose had pulled his pistol, and went inside, and was now making his way back out. There was no sign of her father, and by the look on the faces of the men, she knew something was terribly wrong in the room. She tried to open the door, but the car was locked to prevent an exit.

Ryan walked up to the car, and slung the back door open. He reached inside, and literally yanked Aubrey from the back seat. He took her by the arm, leading her as if he were trying to rush to some sort of scene. Aubrey tried to keep up, but tripped and fell. Ryan held on, pulling her back on to her feet. When they got to the door, Aubrey saw the blood all over the room.

"Wanted to get something off your chest, and just wanted to talk with him?" Ryan was looking directly into her eyes.

Aubrey couldn't believe what she was seeing, the room was covered in blood, and all the furniture was either broken or turned over. The beds were messed up, and the one her father had been sitting on was soaked in blood. She began to get light headed and looked at Ryan. He was still staring right at her.

"There's a dead body up the street we just took away, then we come in here, and see this. You better start telling us what's going on," he scolded her.

Aubrey turned back, and looked at the room. Ryan was still holding her arm with a tight grip so she turned her head the other way and got sick. She bent over in pain as everything was emptied out of her. Ryan let go, but still kept his hand on her back. She couldn't remember ever being that sick in her life, but the sight of all the blood was too much for her. When she was finished throwing up, she stood straight again, and started to cry.

Don had returned from the car, and stood beside the two, "put her back in the car," Ryan told him.

Ryan walked back into the room, passing the manager as he went, "go back to sleep, if we need anything from you, well come get you," he told him.

Ryan started up the stairs at the end of the rooms, and went to the first room that the manager said someone was in. The room was located directly above Ben's room, so he knocked on the door, and waited for the occupant to answer. After a long wait, a woman came to the door, opening it just enough that Ryan could see one of her eyes and her lips.

"What chu want?" she said in a strong southern drawl.

Ryan showed her his badge, and then put it back in his pocket, "did you hear anything from downstairs?" he asked her.

"Damn right I did, some kinda fight going on down der", she told Ryan." There was some woman, and a man, they was yelling, and screaming at each other somethin horrible. Both of them was making all kind of noise, and cussing like there ain't gonna be a tomorrow."

"What time was that?"

"I ain't got a clock in here. Busted I think, but it musta been about a half hour ago."

"Was there only one man, and one woman yelling?"

"Sounded like the same two to me," she said. "One of dem left right after I heard some things breakin in da room, think it was the woman, but I didn't look, it scared me too bad. I just sat in here, hoping someone would come and stop whatever was going on."

"Did you see anything else?"

"No, I told you, I sat here in the dark, them people was crazy, and I don't want no part of crazy. Been in the corner of this room ever since."

Ryan thanked the lady, and went back down to the car. If this indeed did happen about 30 minutes ago, that would put Aubrey coming out of the room right about the time the police arrived on the scene for the murder up the street, or shortly thereafter. It was looking more, and more like there may be something to what Don believed. What bothered him if in fact Aubrey was involved, what did she do with all the blood?

Forensics was arriving on the scene as Ryan got back down to the room. The two men came in, and started processing the evidence in the room. Ryan stood back, and watched for a few short minutes, and then went back to the car. Don was leaning on the front fender talking with one of the ambulance drivers that had come with forensics.

"Lets take her back to the station, we need to see her in the light, and ask her some questions," he said. "I think we're going to have one very long day my friend, a very long day indeed."

Chapter Eleven

Sara Temple drove slowly toward her house thinking of things she never would have imagined would run through her head. Aubrey was in trouble, more than the problems she had divulged to her and Amy earlier. It seemed likely she would be arrested, and Sara tried hard to find a reason in her mind that she shouldn't be. The events over the last two days all seemed to point to Aubrey, and she and Amy were aware of some sort of motive for the crimes. Sara wanted to find out if the other men killed had anything to do with Ben, or if it was just a coincidence they were killed in the same place Aubrey happened to be. It troubled her, and it troubled Amy too. The two of them hadn't spoken since they left the scene with the two detectives.

"Amy," her mother started to say, "You're her best friend. Do you know anything about any of this, or anything about what Aubrey told us tonight?"

Amy didn't answer; she continued to look out the window at the cold whisking by. She was in a semi state of shock, and the question her mother had just asked didn't deserve a response. She had known Aubrey most of her life, and she never suspected her father could, or would do that to her. She must be living in hell every night at that house, and Amy felt completely sorry for her. She also felt a twinge of guilt over never noticing Aubrey had this sort of problem.

"Amy, please tell me, did you know anything about any of this?" her mother asked again.

Amy never looked away from the window, "no," was all she said.

She could feel the cold on her face from the glass, and it felt good to her skin. It was the kind of cold that seeped through the glass, and tickled at your skin, touching the inner child in you. She was thinking about what the police were doing to Aubrey, and how her mother wouldn't even help her. They were both there. They could have given them the alibi Aubrey needed to get out of the detective's clutches. Deep inside she knew that Aubrey wasn't part of any of these murders, and the police were wrong for taking her to the station.

The two women turned into the driveway just as the sun started to part the darkness, and show the light of day. With dawn on the horizon, Amy felt as if she had been awake for days.

"Can I stay home from school today?' She asked her mom, without looking at her.

"Of course," Sara told her. "We'll sleep for a while, and then go to the police station, to see if we can help Aubrey, will that be all right?"

Amy looked at her mother, and thought how kind it was of her to think about how she felt after all. They walked arm in arm to the door, and went inside. Amy wished her father were there, that he hadn't died, and left them both. He always knew what to do, and what to say to make her feel better. She missed him terribly. She felt alone many times over the years since his death, but never as alone as she did now. She thought that he could explain to her why someone would do this to his own daughter, why a man would endanger his own blood that way. She separated from her mother, and went to get something to drink.

Sara had never wanted a cup of coffee so bad in her life, so she went to the kitchen to brew some up prior to crawling into bed. She felt exhausted to the point of collapse, and she could see that Amy was the same way.

While she sat at the breakfast bar in the kitchen she switched on the television, while Amy got a drink of orange juice from the refrigerator, at the same time. The morning news was already underway, reporting about the night's happenings in the Middle East, and all the bad things that had happened in the obscurity of darkness. Both stopped when they heard the name, Bobby Minor, from the reporter. Sara turned the sound up quickly.

"Mr. Minor was found by a passerby in the street about 3 a.m.," the reporter said. "He was taken to the University of Tennessee where he was pronounced dead, an autopsy will be performed to determine the exact cause of death. A suspect is in custody, seventeen-year-old Aubrey Hendrickson of Knoxville, is being held for questioning at this time."

Sara was surprised that they had named her as a suspect so quickly.

"On a related note," the reporter continued, "Ms. Hendrickson's father, Ben Hendrickson is missing from a hotel room the police had provided for him after yesterday's slaying of Dr. Charles Cranston. Dr. Cranston was found murdered in Mr. Hendrickson's home yesterday afternoon."

A picture of Ben Hendrickson appeared on the screen, an old picture that had to be taken long before the booze had caught up with him.

"If anyone has information regarding Mr. Hendrickson, please call the Knoxville Police Department" the reporter went on to his next story.

Sara switched off the TV, and looked at Amy standing in the kitchen. She was staring blankly at the TV screen, and her drink was pouring out of the glass onto the floor. She looked as though she was past the point of crying or screaming. All she had left out of the emotional day was silence.

"Amy!" her mother said loudly.

"Where could her father be?" Amy blurted out. "Aubrey didn't do anything to him or those other men, I know she didn't!"

Amy dropped the glass on the floor, and ran to her room. Sara stood there for a moment looking in the direction that her daughter went, and then picked up the broken glass pieces off the floor.

Sara had never seen Amy so upset. Even when her father died, she cried, and there was anger in the situation, but this was true panic on her daughters face. Sara threw the glass in the trash, and sat back down, the phone rang.

"Mrs. Temple," Detective Rose's voice was on the other end of the line, "can you come down to the station?"

"Of course," she said.

"Mrs. Temple, please come alone if that's possible."

Sara sat back on her chair, and thought about how tired she really was. It was partially a physical exhaustion, but an emotional and mental fatigue overpowered the ache in her bones. She got up, and went to Amy's room. Amy was on her bed, her head buried in a pillow, but already taking the deep breaths that accompanies sleep.

Horrible things happen to children everyday, but no child should have to endure the pain of losing a Father, such as Amy did. Nor should they have to think that existence depends on that of a perverted Father, such as Aubrey did. Sara thought that the strong bond the two shared was perhaps founded in that premise.

She turned, and grabbed her keys, and readied for the trip to the police station. She hoped she could stay awake in the car until she got there. The happenings of the past twenty-four hours were lining up quickly to release into a blur of sleep. She got in her car, and pulled out of the drive.

Don Breeding sat at his desk, and waited for Mrs. Temple to arrive. They had questioned Aubrey, for a short time when she fell ill and had to be taken to the restroom. They hadn't been able to get one answer from her; all she did was keep her head down on the table. Ryan was in with the Chief, trying to explain why they brought the young girl back for questioning. Something didn't seem right to either one of them. They both had theories, but both went in different directions. Don picked up the phone, and dialed the coroner's photographer. Don wanted to see if there were any pictures of the scene where the victim had been found dead, shots of the crowd is what he was looking for more than anything. Both Ryan and Don had noticed the well-dressed woman watching the events unfold. She looked so far out of place neither one of them could get her out of their mind.

The female uniformed officer brought Aubrey back from the restroom. She looked absolutely exhausted, and now her stomach was acting up. The exhaustion made her look as though she would need a hospital bed, not one just to sleep in. She sat in the chair next to Don, and again laid her head on his desk.

"We've called Mrs. Temple to come and get you," he told her.

"Please stay with her until this is all cleared up, so we know where you are. If you hear from your father, we need to know."

"Do you think he's dead?" she asked without raising her head.

Don paused before he answered her. He thought to himself she had innocence about her, a fragrance of not knowing what happened to Mr. Hendrickson, and he probably believed that part of the story. But the other three men, he knew there was something that tied them all together. It was only a matter of time before they found out what it was.

"We don't know yet, and I've learned speculation on those matters only gets you in trouble."

Ryan walked out of the office across from them, and walked over to the desk. He pulled up a chair from the desk next to Don's, and looked at Aubrey.

"Did you know the man that was killed last night?" he asked her.

"I don't want to answer any more questions, please," she said with begging tone in her voice.

"I don't want to ask many more, Aubrey. This is important to all of this; did you know the man that was killed this morning?"

"Yes, yes, yes," she said. "I knew him; he was a friend of my Dad's."

Both detectives looked at each other, "a friend of your Dad's?" Don said. "Do you know if he had seen your father before he was killed?"

"I was with my father just before you picked me up, I didn't see him then, and I don't know if he was with him before I got there."

Sara walked into the room, and Aubrey heard her ask another officer where the two detectives were located. Aubrey lifted her head, and immediately stood up.

"Aubrey, you go home and get some sleep, we'll contact you as soon as we hear anything about your father."

Sara walked up and put her arms around Aubrey. Aubrey hugged her hard, squeezing her as if she were her own mother.

"Can we speak to you for just a moment Mrs. Temple?" Ryan asked.

The uniformed officer that had taken Aubrey to the restroom stepped forward, and guided Aubrey, to another chair. Sara sat down at the desk with a disgusted look on her face both detectives read quite clearly.

"You and your daughter know something about all of this, don't you?" Ryan asked.

"I know you brought a teenager to this station without the permission of her father, or any adult, I know that."

"Lets start over, Mrs. Temple, I assure you we are trying to help her, her father is missing, and someone he knew was killed up the street from where he was staying. Aubrey was there, as well as the two other murders, you tell me if that doesn't seem a little too coincidental."

Sara just looked at both of them, "the man that was killed came to my house not long before he was killed. He asked for Aubrey by name, but I wouldn't let her see him, or let him see her. He was drunk, and was talking crazy. Stuff about loving Aubrey, and wanting to spend the rest of his life with her. I told him to leave, and he did. Afterward, Aubrey told us he was a man her father let molest her, a sort of selling of his daughter if you will. I don't know if there was any money, but the bastards were doing things to this young girl that should not have been done. That's really all I know about the man that was killed."

Both Don and Ryan listened as Sara spilled everything Aubrey had told her, and Amy earlier. When she was finished they sat back in their chairs, and studied the room, not looking at anything in particular. They both knew they finally had some connection to the two men. Ryan was about to say something when one of the lab technicians came into the room, and headed for Ryan's desk.

"Detective Rose?" he asked. "We have some news about your hotel room."

Ryan stood up, and went to the other side of the room with the technician, the young man looked excited, and about to burst with information.

"You know all the blood you thought was in the room?"

Ryan was losing his patience quickly, "get on with it," he said.

"Well, it wasn't blood, it was the blood they use in theater, similar to the same fake blood kids use during Halloween, and some red food coloring thrown in for good measure," he stood with a puzzled but thrilled look on his face.

"Fake blood?" Ryan asked in astonishment.

Ben Hendrickson used fake blood to make it look as though he had been taken, or worse, killed. He had gone through a great deal of trouble to make the room look as though he was in trouble, and according to Aubrey, he had done it after she had left him there. Ryan motioned for the uniformed officer to bring Aubrey back over to his desk.

"I think your father is very much alive," he told her. "The blood in the room was planted there to make it look like he was in some sort of trouble. Why would he go to that kind of trouble?"

Aubrey looked at him, and thought maybe he was just trying to get her to confess to something she hadn't done. He was trying some sort of trick to get a confession out of her. She had seen the room, it was a mess, blood everywhere, with the furniture turned over, and the bed soaked in the unmistakable crimson of violence. She couldn't trust him yet, she couldn't tell him the truth yet, there had to be more time before any of that could happen.

Chapter Twelve

She stood in the back of the small crowd, watching the police try to figure out what had happened to the man on the sidewalk. She was dressed in a pinstripe business dress, and black heels, very high end for the neighborhood she was in. Several of the people that were present looked as if they were homeless, or at least their home might be one of the many bars in the area.

The man in front of her was dirty, and smelled like he hadn't had a bath in years. He clung to a shopping cart like it was his only possession. She moved to the other side of him, covering her lips and nose, so she wouldn't inhale anymore of his scent. When she moved, she noticed the other policemen were taking a young girl into a car and driving away. Both men looked at her, and she looked away, trying hard to blend in with the few people out at this time of night. She knew her dress would bring attention to the police so she tried again to hide behind one of the homeless standing there. She also wanted to look at the girl, she hadn't seen her in years, and she marveled at how she had grown, but with the police directly by her, it was almost impossible to see her face. She turned, and walked down the street.

It wasn't far to where she was holding Ben Hendrickson. The plan had worked so far. After Aubrey had left the room, she went inside without even a knock on the door. Ben was surprised, but his state of inebriation made it incredibly easy to get the drug administered into his arm. She really didn't care if it was his arm, or his posterior end she stuck the needle in, hurting him a little was just a perk to the situation. She managed the arm and a satisfying squeal when she jabbed it as deep as she could. Coupled with the booze, the drug had worked quickly. It didn't knock him out completely, but added to his sense of drunkenness. She managed to get him into her car, and drive him away with as little fan-fare as possible.

Before the injection, he managed a few well-placed verbal jabs at her, and they knocked over some of the furniture. She felt it was probably a convincing factor when the police did arrive. She added the fake blood in the room to throw off some of the investigation. She knew it would be obvious to the police after they looked at the blood, but it gave here valuable minutes. If he wouldn't have been drunk, she would have never pulled off the abduction, but she knew that with Aubrey placing his guilt where it belonged, he would be unable to resist the bottle.

She walked the short distance to the apartment where Ben was lying on the floor, tied up like the pig he was. He was still passed out, and hadn't moved at all. She went into the bathroom, and got a very cold glass of water. She sat on the bed, and thought about throwing it on him. She had blindfolded him, tied him, and left him there on the floor before she went to see the remains of Bobby Minor. Now she wasn't sure if she wanted him awake yet. Perhaps it would be better for him to remain passed out for a while longer. The only reason she wanted to wake him was to tell him of her next move, the move that would prove Aubrey innocent, and put the trail somewhere else. Three down and three to go. Of course Ben's death would be the most gratifying. She hadn't decided what she would do to him as of yet though.

She decided to drink the water instead of dumping on Ben, he would be out for a few more hours, and she would be able to go make sure Aubrey was still at the police station. She grabbed her coat, and headed out one more time.

Aubrey and Sara Temple, walked out from the police station, and headed for the car. Both had been very quiet as they came down the elevator to the lobby. Neither seemed to want the silence broken. It was a sunny, but cold day again. The gray had made way for sunshine, and clear skies around Tennessee. All of the splendors of the Smoky Mountains came out when the sun shone, the smell, the openness of the state, everything one could love about an area. Aubrey took in the sun on her face for a few short moments, and then finished walking to the car with Sara.

"Do you think my father would have faked this, Sara?" she asked as they sat in the car.

"I'm not sure of what I think yet, this is certainly more than I thought I'd have to ponder ever in my life."

"He was alive when I left, and he was still in the room. I don't understand how someone could have gotten to him so quickly after I went out on the street."

Sara backed the car out of the parking space, and started toward her house. She desperately needed to sleep, and she knew Aubrey did too. She thought of Amy still at home in her bed, hoping there were some good dreams mixed in her head today. Before she got the car out of the parking lot, Aubrey was nodding her head, trying to keep her eyes open long enough to make it to the house.

Inside the station, Ryan watched out the window as the two women walked to their car. His mind was busy trying to figure out the happenings of the last two days. Several things didn't add up, both with the murder victims, and with the suspect they just had in custody. Over the past few years, he and Don, had become very proficient at interviewing suspects, and breaking them had become what many thought was a specialty. He was inclined to believe the girl, believe she was where she said she was, and she didn't have anything to do with the disappearance of her father. What he couldn't come to grips with was the connection between her, her father, and two of the three victims. His curiosity was also peaked by the woman hanging around the crime scene. He turned around, and saw Don sitting at his desk with the same far away look on his face.

"Did you see the woman at the crime scene?" he asked him. "The one that so well dressed."

"It's funny you would ask me about her, I was just sitting here thinking about that. She looked a little out of place, didn't she?"

"You know, she was there, but it looked to me like she was trying to not be there. Kind of disappear into the crowd standing around."

Don sat up straight in his chair, "I got the same feeling, like she wanted us to see her, but at the same time, for us not to notice her."

"You know we still have the Cranston situation, could that have been the good doctor's wife?"

"I didn't get a good look at her face, but I think we need to go see her, and find out why she refused the autopsy and removed her husband so quickly," Don, told Ryan.

The chief came out of his office, as the two were getting ready to see if Congresswoman Cranston had returned from her trip yet, "both of you have a visitor on her way up," he said. "Dr. Cranston's widow just came in, and wants to see the detectives in charge. Remember Ryan, she's a very popular figure in Sevier County, and lets not read about any of this in the news."

Mrs. Cranston came out of the elevator just as he finished. She was a tall good-looking woman. Not one you would call beautiful, but regal and classy. She had dark hair that was put up, and she wore a dark business suit. She looked extremely conservative, and not a woman in mourning for her husband. She came with two other men at her side, one with a notebook, and one that was undoubtedly her attorney. She kept her head high, as if to tell the others she was in charge. She made no mistake of portraying a helpless woman. Her demeanor was just as crisp as her wardrobe and her unmistakable walk of confidence.

"Mrs. Cranston, I'm Detective Ryan Rose, and this is my partner Don Breeding, we were just coming to see you," he stuck his hand out in greeting.

Mrs. Cranston continued to walk without acknowledging the greeting, or introduction. She walked into an office at the end of the hallway along with her two companions, and stood there waiting for the two detectives to follow.

Ryan and Don looked at each other, and Don nodded with uncertainty.

"I understand from the coroner you two had some questions about why I took my husband last night?" she said in a matter of fact voice.

Ryan came in the room, and closed the door behind him and Don, "it is a little unusual for someone to come and get a body before an investigation begins," he said.

"I assure you sir, I had the approval of your superiors. Otherwise I would not have done it."

"I realized you have some power Mrs. Cranston, but my question is, why? It seems to me you would be interested why your husband, a respected doctor in the community, would be killed on a pool table at a patient's house. Taking the body, and having it cremated could stop us from getting very important evidence."

"Detective Rose, my husband's death is no one's business, especially the media, and that's how I see this. The sooner I can get it out of the newspapers, the sooner I can get on with my life. I know that my husband had, let us say, questionable affairs with underage women. I don't need that to come out in the public eye, for his sake and mine. There's a lot more at stake than your little murder case here."

Ryan's temper started to flare immediately. The arrogance of the woman was overwhelming. To him, it seemed as if she thought this was all a big joke. Murder was no –little thing-, as she called it, and the fact Knoxville was embroiled in one of the biggest murder cases in history was something he thought she should be very concerned with.

Don saw that Ryan was on the verge of letting her have his wrath, "where were you last night?" Don asked her.

"I wasn't in town if that's what you mean," she turned, and started to walk back out into the outer offices, Ryan stepped in front of her.

"Congresswoman Cranston, it's not your decision to just leave this questioning, we have three murders here in a matter of hours. You know that doesn't normally happen here in Knoxville. Your husband was brutally murdered, and he didn't just die on the side of the street of natural causes. Now you can cooperate with us or we will make sure that the media gets some sort of story about this entire affair, or we can do it the easy way, it's your decision."

Her determination stood out in every vein on her, she glared into the eyes of the detective, he obviously didn't know who she was, "detective, unless I'm under arrest, you have no right to keep me here," she turned, and looked at her attorney, who nodded in agreement. "I've answered all the questions you posed to me, now if you will excuse us; I have to go to my husband's funeral."

She strutted out the door, and down the hall, both Don and Ryan watched intently as she walked away, Don noticed her bright red nails as she slung her wrap around her shoulders.

Ryan thought to himself, funeral, that's awfully quick after a death isn't it?

Chapter Thirteen

There once was a large department store located on the outskirts of Knoxville vacated for a move to a larger superstore location. It had remained empty for a couple of years, and its closing had almost ruined the remainder of the stores in the strip center. There was nothing special about the center, they're everywhere in every city, but this one had a unique entrance, and exit. When you drove into it, you drove down a long elevated road to the center. It was the entrance to the strip center that allured a new tenant to its new home, and she knew the owner would be there waiting for plans to be delivered so they could discuss plans for his new operation.

Harold Massey stood by himself in the huge area that used to house all the things one could buy. He was always amazed at the size of the store, and wondered how he could ever fill it up. His dream of having a large sports store was slowly happening, thanks to an inheritance, and some shrewd banking maneuvers. He moved his large frame back and forth to music playing on a radio in a distance, unknowingly moving his lips to the words, and swaying in a dancing motion. If he thought someone was watching, he would certainly stop the swaying; his body wasn't anything one would want to see in a dance. Maybe twenty years, and two hundred pounds ago, but now things had changed dramatically in all directions.

In front of him was a set of blueprints with the *Knoxville News Sentinel* sprawled out on top of them. The headline had peeked his interest when he was in line for coffee, so he slapped the money down, and hurriedly came back to wait for the contractor. There was a man found on the street not far from where he lived so he thought the article would be of interest. His mood changed with every word, and the reality of knowing another person that was murdered brought him back from the joyful art of the music.

It was something he never thought about, at least not consciously. He read the name one more time, Bobby Minor, one of his workers that did occasional plumbing, and drywall work. He was an independent, so Harold tried to funnel as much work to him as he could. They had talked several times, and eventually they became friends. Bobby had shared an intimate moment one night while they were having a few beers, so Harold helped realize one of his fantasies. It was that fantasy and those secrets that kept their friendship going. He settled back on his heels, the shock showing on his face as his swaying, and singing stopped. He read through the text one more time. It wasn't that they liked each other so much, it was the sharing of the secrets they had that made him bow his head in sorrow.

The rest of the article was the same as any article written about a mystery murder. At the end, the reporter had put the small paragraph about Ben Hendrickson missing from the hotel room, not far from where Bobby had been found.

He looked around the spacious room, peering into nothingness for some sort of reality check. In the past two days, he had lost three friends, and another missing. Nothing could be that coincidental, he was sure of that. All of these men were together at one time or another. Living was always on their mind, dying was never part of the conversation.

He reached for his cell phone, lying next to the paper, and dialed a number quickly, "Roger," he paused. "Yea I just read it, we need to get together and talk about this," he said into the phone. "No, I didn't have any idea; I just saw it in the paper along with Ben's disappearance. We'll meet at the restaurant somewhere around eleven. Call Scooter and tell him to be there too," he hung up and looked around the building again, and then at his watch.

Roger Fallon was one of Harold's early business partners, long before he ever came into money, or ever thought he would. He was a retired airline pilot that took a buyout, and retirement, and had helped Harold early on, for a fee of course. Roger's ability to work his way into your business was almost legendary in the area, but Harold had learned early with every dollar there was a higher price to pay. Not long after the partnership was formed, Harold found additional financing, and bought Roger out before any real hard feelings surfaced. Since then they had been friends, not real close, but they shared a common desire that made them stay close, much like he and Bobby. Roger was calculating, and overbearing, and his way with people would always need improving, but under the gruff exterior probably laid a heart, although no one Harold knew had found it yet. He was short in stature, and in patience, and a few people that knew him had told Harold he suffered from what they called little man's disease. He would try to command a room with loud talk, and open criticisms of anyone that may be having a bad day. Most people just brushed him aside, but some took hard offense to his remarks, so he had spent more than a few days in the emergency room in his lifetime. The beatings and verbal assaults never seemed to deter his demeanor, nor change his approach to how he treated those around him. Harold figured someday he would hear about him through the evening news as a four second headline for death.

Scooter, on the other hand, was a wild and whimsical soul that only looked for living, and lived for looking. Anything in a skirt could become his next conquest. His ability to light up a room showed wherever they traveled together. The biggest vice he had was the young girls he constantly chased, and his love for beer and a party. It wasn't uncommon to see him down a twelve-pack before they got to the bar. He had been arrested for DUI six or seven times, and would never own another driver's license, the state had seen to that early in his life. He hung on to Roger and Harold because they were always headed to the same place, and could afford him the ride. He liked being around them because of Roger's command for power, and Harold's desire to keep everyone happy with another drink. He followed others rather than lead them. Leadership was something he felt needed to be left to those like

Roger. Scooter didn't have a dime to his name, and Roger liked keeping that kind of company. People like Scooter always needed for something, and Roger could get back what he lent in spades. Scooter was especially close to Bobby Minor, but the two had quarreled several times about Aubrey, after Bobby confessed he was in love with her. Scooter told him many times that falling in love with her couldn't be the answer to his problems, only the beginning. Harold thought to himself that he was probably right, now he was dead. Scooter hopped from one woman to another and the younger the better. His ventures started in bars, looking for anyone he thought might be underage, and offer to buy them a drink, or get them into a nightclub that they couldn't buy their way past the bouncer. He was loud, and sometimes obnoxious, but his lighthearted way made just about everyone that ever met him laugh.

Harold started to walk to the back of the store, and check on the few workers he had going this morning. They had arrived just before he did, and had started on the work on their own. He thought that was a good sign, but he still needed to keep an eye on them, for his own piece of mind. The place was huge, and with no merchandise in the building, it even looked bigger. He thought sometimes this undertaking was probably not the best thing for him, but the dream lived within him, and he was going to see it through. He stopped once to catch his breath, and look at some of the lighting that had been installed wrong the day before, as he did, he heard the front door open, and close again.

He had been waiting for a contractor, so there was no hurry for him to turn around, and see who had entered, but when he finally did, no one was there. He started back to the table to get the cell phone he had forgotten when he walked away. The walk through a warehouse this size wasn't great for someone light on their feet, and when you weighed over four hundred pounds, forgetting something required a thought or two, before going back and forth. When he reached it, he was already breathing heavy, and sweating as if he hadn't showered for a week. He turned to work his way to the workers in the back, when he heard a noise up in the front of the store.

"John, is that you?" he called out. "C'mon, I ain't got all day, I need to be somewhere in a little while, and we got things to go over."

There was no reply from anyone, but there was now a banging on something up by where his electrical boxes were being located. He decided to make his way to the front, and see who had come in.

The electricians had put a temporary wall up in the front so they could do welding while others worked in the store, it was far from sound proof, but Harold figured if someone was behind it, they probably couldn't hear him. He went to the wall, and looked around the corner. By the fuse boxes was a young man with a portable CD headset on, working on the wires as he listened to music. Harold felt relieved, and turned back around to get back to the rear of the building. He chuckled to himself, and thought maybe he was getting a touch of paranoia, after all that happened this week.

He walked halfway to the back, took a few seconds to catch his breath, and then walked the rest of the way. When he got there, the workers in the back room greeted him with the working of hammers, and screw guns as they got the inside walls put up for the drywall people to come in tomorrow. He thought of Bobby, and how he would have to find someone to replace him soon, he couldn't wait very long.

His inspection was short, and he went to his truck parked in the rear of the building, got in and headed down to the restaurant to meet Scooter, and Roger. As he drove around the front of the building, he noticed a well dressed lady going in the front doors, good looking enough that he thought about turning around to see what she wanted, but decided if it was important, she would be there when he got back, or find him later. He drove out of the front, and went down to get something to eat.

He wasn't sure what he wanted to say to his two friends, but this whole thing was getting pretty weird. The police were on pins and needles. Serial murders weren't something this town was used to. The news media was eating it up with reports almost hourly on the radio, and a complete dominance of the story on the television. One of the reasons people moved to Knoxville was because of the low crime rate, and its reputation for having some of the friendliest folks around. This wasn't going to do anything for the tourist trade if it lasted much longer. He tried several times to rehearse some sort of speech, but in the end decided that just a regular conversation would get the ball rolling.

When he pulled into the parking lot of the regular restaurant where they ate, he noticed the other two had already arrived, and were seated. Scooter was giving the waitress a hard time about something she was wearing, and Roger was talking on his cell phone, as he usually was. Roger motioned for him to come on over, and closed his phone, shoving it into his pocket.

"We'll have the buffet today darlin," he told the waitress, "and bring us all some sweet tea; the sweeter the better."

Harold sat on the opposite side of the two, taking up space where two seats should be. His friends would always sit where there was enough room for Harold, and always put his back to the door so he wouldn't see the reaction a large man made from the other customers, as they came in the door. He knew people looked at him as if he were a freak, but he appreciated that his friends cared enough to at least try to hide it from him.

"Ok, Roger, you know about Bobby and Ben, Scooter, did you know about Bobby being killed last night?"

"Yea, I found out this morning," he replied with his head down. "I didn't think all of it was connected though, until Roger called. We all knew Cranston, and Williams too, so what does it all mean?"

Roger fidgeted against the window, as he looked out into the street, "we have to go to the police and tell them the connection," he said quietly, not turning away from the window.

Scooter looked at him with revulsion, "how can we do that, we waltz in there, and tell them we've been having sex with a young girl her daddy sells us, hell, just open the cell, we can walk right in."

"Keep your voice down," Harold scolded Scooter. "We can't go to the police; we have to find a way to get this taken care of ourselves. First, we need to find out where Ben is, that's going to help us find out who's behind all this."

Roger continued to look out the window, staring at nothing in particular. When Harold finished scolding the both of them, Scooter got up, and went to the buffet bar, and started getting his food. It didn't seem as though anything bothered Scooter. He dismissed things as easy as overhearing boring conversation.

Harold looked at Roger, "we have to stick together on this Roger, all of us need to keep in close touch, and if we see anything that may be unusual, we need to let each other know. If you ask me, I think the girl is involved somehow. She's either told someone about us, or she's the one doing it. Whatever it is, we can't go to the police, and we can't just sit around waiting to die either."

Roger just nodded without a response. Scooter came back with a full plate of chicken, with potatoes, and other food piled high. He started in on the chicken right away, not taking any time to talk, or ask what the conversation was about.

When he had swallowed he spoke up, "hell guys, I think that little girl knows something, don't you? She seemed to be getting a little feisty the last time I saw her. You ought to go see her Harold, find out what she's been up to," he barely stopped chewing to talk.

Harold thought about Scooter's suggestion for a minute. Scooter wouldn't be any good at looking into the circumstances, and Roger was too deep into saving his own ass to even consider the move. Harold thought the idea might not be a bad one at that.

"You might be right, Scooter," he said. "I'll go over there tonight, and see what I can find out. With Ben missing, she should be home alone, and we can talk about everything there."

The three men agreed that Harold would handle Aubrey, and then meet in a couple of days to talk about what he had discovered. There was a sense of relief among the men as they ate lunch.

Harold drove back to the warehouse with a new outlook on what was happening. He was having trouble hiding the fact this whole thing scared him, like nothing ever had in his life. His affair with an underage girl had always been in the back of his mind, but he thought nothing would come out of it, with her father involved. He considered that if anyone did find out, Ben would end up taking the brunt of blame, and perhaps his name would never come out. It was something he told himself constantly, more to keep his guilt down than anything. Murder had never entered his mind, and until recently, he didn't think what they were doing could ever come to light. Now, three of the men involved were dead, and the main character was missing. It was unnerving.

He pulled to the back of the store with plenty of day left to get done what was needed in his quest for his new store. When he parked, he noticed the vans had been there for the men working in the back were gone. He assumed they had left for lunch, there were several fast-food spots close by, and so he didn't worry about them. He went inside, and immediately he was greeted with darkness. This was unusual for the warehouse, lights were always on somewhere, but now everything was off. The back door closed behind him, so he instantaneously turned back around, and reopened it. The light flooded in like liquid as he found something to block the door open, while he found the electrical problem. He fumbled past some other doors, and went for the main breaker box located down a dark hallway. Light from the open doorway was little help, as he made his way to the room with the breaker box in it, so he used his hands to run along the wall, and help him find the way. He hoped there was only a small problem, and the workers didn't go because of some sort of outage in the building. He remembered, as he worked his way down the hall, there was a young man working on the electrical box, just before he left for lunch.

He stopped, and decided to turn back to the door he had left open. He would find a flashlight in his truck, and go into the main showroom to see if the young man had some sort of trouble while working in there. He flipped on the flashlight, and headed for the showroom portion of the huge building. Harold went into the showroom, with the light from the front windows helping somewhat, as he trudged across the tile floor. He stopped by the table, where his plans were still scattered across with the newspaper on top of them, to catch his breath, and then continued. There wasn't any movement by the partitions the electricians had set up, and the darkness was more prevalent in that area. He displayed the flashlight over to where the young man had been. When he got closer, he called out thinking he might be able to get his attention in the dark, and perhaps have an answer before he had to go behind the wall. When he didn't get an answer, he continued on using the flashlight stream to lead the way.

He reached the end of the wall, and started to go around to get a look at the work area. When he did, he noticed his foot slipped just a bit, like he had stepped in some sort of liquid. He turned the flashlight downward, and looked at the floor. He was standing in what looked like blood, thick and crimson, and spreading out on the floor in a slow river of silence. Harold took two more steps, and shined the light on the wall.

Leaning on the wall was the young man, his earphones still around his head, the wire dangling along side of him with the CD player swaying freely. He was still facing the wall where he had been working. Someone had pierced a long rod through the middle of him, almost dead center between his shoulder blades, pinning him to the fresh drywall. A stream of his blood was flowing down the wall, and on to the tile floor.

Harold couldn't take the flashlight off of the young man, standing as if he were waiting for someone to help him get away from the wall. His head was at very painful angle.

The sight of the young man took Harold by surprise, and he dropped the light. It crashed on the floor, losing what little light he had. The panic was rising in his chest, and throat, and his head was starting to spin with a fearful anticipation.

He turned, and started to walk as fast as he could back to the rear of the store, his huge body lunging up and down, as he consciously tried to pick his heavy legs up, putting one in front of the other. He had to get to his phone, and let someone know what was going on here. The darkness was surrounding him now, and he hurriedly looked for the light from the windows. He was starting to breath heavy as he tried to get away from the wall, and the young man leaning there in his deadly pose. His breathing grew heavier, and heavier as he tried to run. He realized that he didn't seem to be getting to the area he was looking for, and thought maybe he was going in circles. He wanted to stop and rest. Then catch his breathe, and go on, but he needed to get out of the room.

He kept running, or something that resembled a run. Then he noticed a bright light pointed at him. It moved slowly across the floor in his direction. He couldn't see who was behind it, but decided to turn around, and go the other way. His breathing was now laboring so hard that he was starting to get dizzy from the lack of oxygen his huge body starved for. He stopped for a second with his back to the light, thinking that if whoever was behind reached him, he may have a chance, on the other hand it may be the killer.

His body was telling him to stop and catch his breath, but he kept moving. Suddenly he felt a sharp pain in his left arm. It traveled to his chest, and he grabbed the middle of his body, squeezing what he thought must be his heart. He fell to the floor, landing on his side with pain so great that it took his sight away. He turned on to his back, and felt two more sharp pains in his chest. He could feel the heat from the light shining directly on his face. He realized the person was directly on top of him, watching as the life inside him slipped away into darkness. He tried to speak, but his words were only whispers in his own head. Many of his thoughts that were intended for this person to hear weren't, and never would be. Then everything went completely black as he felt the pain in his chest subside. He closed his eyes with his final thoughts slipping into the eternity that he was convinced was death.

She stood over him for a few seconds waiting to see if the huge mound of flesh on the floor would move again. The flashlight was trained on his face, and she saw all of his muscles relax. When his face lost some of the shape that life gives, she took the rose from her pocket, bent down and placed it between his legs, and mumbled to herself, "remember the innocence you stole."

The walk out to the car was one of satisfaction, maybe the most satisfying walks she had ever made. She savored this kill, and as she walked away she thought to herself, only two left to go. She smiled big, showing her teeth, almost in a laugh. She thought to herself that if anyone were watching, they would think she was close to being insane.

Chapter Fourteen

Harold woke up for only a few seconds. He opened his eyes, and looked at what he thought was an ambulance attendant. He couldn't believe he was alive; that he had actually lived through that nightmare. Standing over him was a nice face, the face of someone that told him to go back to sleep, he would be at the hospital very soon. He spoke in what sounded like slow motion to Harold, but it was understandable. Harold tried to speak, but he realized he couldn't, so he did as he was told with no objection. He closed his eyes again, and went to sleep.

Ryan stood in the parking lot, looking at the ambulance as it started away to Baptist Hospital. The man in it would probably live, but he was far from being out of the woods. It seemed that it was a lucky break for him, the heart attack was bad, very bad, and it would take him some time before he would be able to lead the life he was used to, but he was alive. Ryan thought to himself that the man would probably look a bit different when he emerged from the halls of the hospital. He was sure there would be a lot less weight hanging from his bones when they were done with him. Ryan thought to himself one more time, how lucky the man was to be alive.

The victim inside the store was a different story, he had died almost instantly, and whoever hit him did it from behind, and without warning. There was no sign of a struggle, just the piece of pipe that had been shoved into his back. He was young, and it was obvious to Ryan the young man had been working when the incident had peeled his life away. He probably didn't have any warning or pain, he was there one second, and gone the next, nothing but death. Ryan shook his head in a wondering fashion, fleeting, that was the word he was thinking of. It never ceased to amaze him. Don came out of the store with a wallet in his hand.

"His name was Gary Dolce, and it looks like he was only working here. His boss is inside, and told me he had sent him to do a few things on electrical items he hadn't finished yesterday. He said he had only been working with him for a short time, so he didn't know much about him except he had just moved here from up north somewhere."

"Who's the big guy?" he asked.

"He's the owner. According to some of the workers inside, he went to lunch, and shortly after he left, the power went out in the building. They figured it would be a little while before it came back on, so all of them went to lunch as well. When they got back there was still no electricity in the back of the store where they were working, so one of them came in the main showroom to look around to see if he could help. That's when he found him," he opened his notebook to look at the name again, "Harold Massey."

Ryan put his head in his hands, and rubbed his forehead, he could feel a headache coming on. He knew they might have just gotten lucky with this guy living through this. The pressure from his superiors was starting to get a little thick. The killings had the city in a near panic. Even though the motive didn't support the fear, many were convinced they were next in line for the madman, or woman to come get them. Serial killers seamed to bring out the worst in a city, including the nut balls. They called the station claiming to either have seen the killer, or be the killer; it depended on the time of day, he supposed.

It was clear the heart attack victim didn't kill the young man. There was no blood on him except his shoes, and a clear path around the room where he ran in a circle. He was trying to flee something or someone it looked like. When a man that size ran, it usually wasn't very far, and Don and Ryan had both deduced he ran to escape something, and when he did, his heart just wasn't up to the task of carrying that kind of load, that fast, or that far.

In addition there was the rose that was placed between his legs. Clearly the killer thought that Mr. Massey was dead, and left her calling card behind, much like the other victims.

"These guys are connected with the other victims," he told Don. "We need to find out if they knew Aubrey, and Ben, and we need to know who else could become a victim. Do we know where he went to lunch?"

"One of the workers in the back said he usually went to the buffet down the street, and he met with some friends there quite a bit. They also said he seemed a little upset when he left today, distracted somewhat. I found his cell phone on the floor inside," he handed Ryan the phone.

Ryan pushed a few buttons, and looked at the man's recent phone call list. Then he handed the phone back to Don, "find out who these last few people are and let's contact them first. I'm getting tired of being a step behind here."

Ryan walked back inside, and went to where they young man was killed. It was a grizzly sight, and it made little sense to Ryan what had happened. The killer had deviated from her normal circumstances, and killed what looked like an innocent bystander. He looked around the room, and especially at the floor. The big man had stepped in the other victim's blood, and by the way it was smeared must have panicked. He ran around in almost a perfect circle, landing just outside where he had started. The panic had caused a heart attack, brought on by a lack of oxygen, at least that's what the EMT had confirmed to him. Whoever wanted him dead had come into the store after Mr. Massey had found the victim, threatened him somehow, and caused him to run.

One thing he was sure of was the murderer thought he was dead, that's why she placed the rose on his crotch. Ryan thought the killer probably set up the big man, knowing he would probably panic, and move himself into the health problem. She obviously wanted to see him suffer. Finally, after all that Aubrey had told them, Ryan thought perhaps they finally had a motive for all the killings, revenge.

Don Breeding hung up his cell phone, and walked back into the store where Ryan was standing. He was alone in the middle of the huge room, staring at the ceiling. Don thought he looked pitiful just standing there. He chuckled to himself knowing none of this was in the least bit funny. He always tried to think of the humor in situations, sometimes it helped to keep him sane in the insane work they did. There was no humor in all of this, and he thought twice before he said anything stupid.

"I've got a name, and address," he said to Ryan as he walked up to him. "He's not far from here, and apparently he had lunch with our victim and another man this afternoon. He's also got a record, petty stuff, nothing serious."

"You know Don, this whole thing stinks," Ryan said without taking his eyes off the ceiling. "I know that this young girl has something to do with this, but this time she's nowhere around. She ties all these guys together."

He looked down at Don, "have we heard anything on her father yet?"

Don shook his head, and the two started to walk out the front of the building. There was crime scene tape around the front entrance, and at the rear. The only people around were some that were mulling, just taking a look at all the happenings. They were people who were already in the shopping center when the crime had occurred, or had slipped through the police line at the top.

When they walked outside, Ryan noticed the woman first, standing about fifty yards away on the opposite side of the parking lot, next to a car. She was well dressed, and again she seemed out of place. Don noticed her about the same time, and stopped on the sidewalk. He reached out, and touched Ryan on the arm, resisting the temptation to point at her.

"I see her too," Ryan said as he motioned Don to keep walking. "She looks like the woman at the other crime scene last night, doesn't she? Keep walking, maybe we can drive over and talk with her."

The two walked to the car. When they were about half way, she turned, got in the car beside her, and quickly drove away. The parking lot was huge so Ryan didn't think they could get to the car, and still be able to follow her, both men broke into a fast walk. When they arrived, and got into the car, Ryan looked in the direction of the exit, the car, and the woman were already gone. They drove to the exit trying to get a glimpse of the car on the street, but it had disappeared. She had definitely been watching what the two detectives were doing. She seemed to be watching so she could see what would come next, and it also seemed as if she knew where they were going to be. They didn't have a clue where she was or what she had to do with this.

The press on the other hand was a different story. When the two detectives drove to the exit, several television trucks, and reporters were standing with pens, and tape recorders in hand waiting impatiently for some sort of statement, met them. The police had formed a staging line to keep everyone off the crime scene area, but most knew the car when Ryan drove out. The press swarmed the car, preventing Ryan from moving to the traffic light, and finding the woman that drove away. His frustration showed as he beat the steering wheel with his hands, finally throwing them up in the air, and simply driving through the crowd, blowing the horn, and making as many gestures with his hands he could think of, until he made his way out to the street.

Don had come up with an address, and phone number of one of the friends Massey had attended his lunch with. Ron decided instead of chasing what might have been a coincidence they should follow up on what seemed to be the only lead they had. They drove in silence for the majority of the trip, both thinking of ways to stop the madness happening in the city, both trying to come up with links to Aubrey, Ben, and the victims.

They arrived at the address, and were greeted with open wrought-iron gates to an estate that was sprawling on the Tennessee hillside. The driveway stretched in front of them hid the house at the end. Bradford Pear trees were on both sides and the shade from them whistled shadows across the landscape. Ryan reached out the window, and touched the intercom button on the brick surrounding the gate.

"Detective Ryan Rose to see Roger Fallon please," he said into the speaker, thinking there might be someone at the other end.

There was no response, only the creaking of the gate as it slowly swayed in wind. Ryan thought it was unusual that this gate would be open for an estate that looked as though it was to be kept private.

"Damn," was all Don could muster.

They pulled in the gate, and went up in front of the door. There, a short man, dressed in a loud shirt and bright slacks, greeted them. Ryan had seen his picture before in the newspaper, but hadn't realized the connection with his name until he saw him. He was a developer that had caused a stir of trouble earlier in the year with a controversial development site. Something about a battle with City Hall he had tried to win in the press, but eventually lost in court.

His face was distraught with worry, and he clearly looked as though he knew why the two detectives were there to talk to him. He paced nervously back and forth in the drive until Ryan, and Don could get the car stopped, and parked safely. He had a cigarette in both hands, having inadvertently lit one before he finished the other.

Ryan smiled to himself, and looked at Don when the car came to a stop, "doesn't look like he has anything to say, does he?" Ryan joked rhetorically.

He strutted to the side of the car before Ryan could open the door, still pacing back and forth like he wasn't sure whether they would get out or not to talk with him.

"You gotta give me protection," he immediately said as Ryan exited the vehicle. "You must get me somewhere that bitch won't be able to find me," he was almost touching Ryan as he invaded what little space Ryan had.

Ryan put his hand out, and tried to get the man to move away, "are you Roger Fallon?' he asked already knowing the answer.

"Yea, and I pay taxes, enough to pay your salaries, you gotta get me somewhere and protect me," he was walking in circles now, almost in a full-fledged panic.

Don reached out and, put his hand on the man's shoulder, "you have to slow down, Mr. Fallon," he said. "Tell us why we have to protect you."

"She's killed four of us, and she's planning on killing the rest as soon as you guys turn your back. She knows where we are, and how to get to us, all she's doing is waiting for you to leave us alone long enough so she can come and get us. I don't know if it's me or Scooter, but I know we're next on her list," he flicked one of the cigarettes away without realizing it was the newest one he had lit.

He stopped pacing, and turned to look at the detectives, glaring his eyes at them, not blinking or moving any longer. He stood there breathless for a few seconds, and then started in once again, "I know she's coming," he said, then turned, and started into the house.

Ryan looked at Don, and indicated for him to try to get in front of him to stop him from getting inside. Don took a few steps, and stopped right in front of Mr. Fallon. Fallon's face was flush with fear and panic; he was talking to himself, and mumbling something about being sorry, sorry for all the things he had done to her. He was sweating, and his face was getting redder by the second.

"Mr. Fallon," Don said in a stern tone. "Please stop and talk to us, if you want protection, you have to tell us what it is you need protection from!"

Don's raising of his voice seemed to get Fallon's attention, and he slowed down, looking to the ground with his head bowed. Both men could tell he was having a hard time keeping the panic at check, but he was trying. Ryan could see it was probably their best chance to talk to him.

"Mr. Fallon, did you have lunch with Harold Massey this afternoon?" Ryan asked as he moved along side of Fallon.

"Yes, and we discussed this very thing, then he went back to work, and that bitch killed him, killed him right there in his own store."

Don looked at him, as directly as someone as tall as he was could to a short man, "he's not dead, Mr. Fallon. He's alive, and at the hospital right now. We don't know if he's going to make it, but he is alive."

Fallon looked up at him with disbelieving eyes, "you need to see something then, something that was in my door when I got back here from lunch and a business meeting."

Fallon started back to his house, and the two detectives followed closely behind. He was walking fast, almost at a trot. When he got to the front door they could see a piece of paper with a picture on it hanging, stuck there with a sharp knife, buried into the wood. Ryan stopped Fallon from grabbing the picture, and went around him quickly.

It was printed on regular paper, like someone had taken it with a digital camera and then run the picture on a printer. It was dark around the edges, but the figure in the middle was bright from the flash. It was Harold Massey, lying face up on the floor, his eyes were closed, and you could see he wasn't able to move anymore. Between his legs was the red rose the killer had left for him. Under the picture, "remember me", was hand written in red pen.

Ryan inspected the picture carefully, then took out a pair of gloves, and removed the knife, dropping the picture into his other hand.

"Have you ever seen this knife?" he asked Fallon without looking up.

"Yea, it's mine, from my kitchen," he answered starting to panic one more time. His face was distorted, and he was becoming increasingly red. His breathing was becoming erratic, and for a quick moment Don thought maybe he too would have a heart attack, and fall over dead right there.

"Calm down, Mr. Fallon," Don said taking his pistol out of his shoulder holster, "have you been inside yet?"

Fallon shook his head no, "I was going inside when you drove up. I didn't know what to do when I saw the picture," he sat down on a bench by the door, "I panicked, and when I saw you two, I hoped you could help me, you are going to help me aren't you? You are going to keep this crazy maniac away from me aren't you?"

"Is anyone else inside?" Ryan asked.

"No, the maid was supposed to be here today, but she couldn't come for some reason, she called me before I went to lunch, and my wife is out of town."

"Open the door, Mr. Fallon," Don said. "See if it's still locked but back away if it is unlocked, we'll open it."

The two detectives readied for the trip inside, one on each side of the door. Fallon reached for the knob, and turned it carefully; the door clicked loudly, and then he pushed it slowly as it started to open. He quickly backed away, and sat back on the bench. Don and Ryan could tell he was spent, completely exhausted from his panic.

They both went inside with guns drawn, stepping quickly around corners, and surveying the rooms as they went into each one. After a few minutes they both came back to the front room with the report of no one being in the home. Ryan put his gun away, and Don followed suit as both men stepped back outside to see how Fallon was doing.

"Did you find anyone?" he asked as the two detectives came through the front door. "Was there anyone inside; is that crazy bitch in there?"

Terror was still confronting Mr. Fallon heavily. He face remained a shade of red, and his breathing was still erratic. It seemed he couldn't get his body to calm down. Ryan sat next to him, and tried to get him to get a grip on himself. Neither one of the detectives wanted to see him throw himself into a heart attack.

"There's no one inside, Mr. Fallon," Ryan told him. "There's no sign of forced entry either, what do you know about this so called "crazy person" you keep talking about?"

The question seemed to take Fallon by surprise, even though he had been spouting about the crazy bitch since they had arrived. He took a few deep breaths, and slowly started showing signs of getting himself back together. His face returned to a somewhat normal hue, and he sat back taking more deep breaths, which seemed to help.

"We were at lunch today, Massey, myself and Scooter. We talked about the murders recently, and decided it was the girl that had to be involved. Massey said he would get in touch with her, and find out what was going on."

"What girl?" Don asked.

"Aubrey Hendrickson, she knows all of us, including all the other victims. Massey thought she had made a pact to kill all of us."

"Now why would a seventeen-year-old girl have any interest in any of you?" Ryan asked him.

Both men could see the dread coming back to Fallon's face. He started to squirm on the bench, and then just shot up, and walked down toward the driveway. He spun around when he was about halfway down the walk. They knew then that he had told them too much and wanted to stop the conversation as quickly as he had started it.

"I want to thank you both for coming by; I don't know what I would have done without you when you came up so quickly. I have several things that I need to prepare for, again thank you for coming and helping me with this."

Ryan thought the man was trying to divert the question, and somehow get both of them to forget what he had just said. He was walking toward their car as if to indicate that they should get into it. They stayed where they were, watching as Fallon stepped towards the car with obvious concern.

"My partner asked you a question, Mr. Fallon," Don said with a certain amount of sarcasm. "Maybe you should thank us for coming with an answer."

"Listen," he said as he turned back toward the house. "I didn't mean anything by that statement, I was just upset over all of this, I don't know what I'm even saying right now, I just need to get going before I miss my appointments today, that's all."

Ryan started walking toward the little man as he stumbled through his words. He was obviously trying to cover up his statement with false appointments and small talk, but Ryan wasn't buying any of it. He stopped directly in front of Fallon, and looked down at him with a glaring gaze that would put anyone into a nervous state.

"One more time, Mr. Fallon, why would a seventeen-year-old be interested in you and your friends? Why would she have any reason for wanting to kill you or the other men?"

Fallon stopped, and hung his head toward the ground. He watched his shoes for what seemed like minutes, but looked back up at Ryan towering over him. His face was flush with embarrassment or shame. Ryan wasn't sure which. His hands were busy with a twisting motion, and sweat was visibly starting to form on his forehead. He started to say something, but stopped, and again looked at the ground. He was stalling, but try as he may, stall wasn't going to make the two detectives go away.

He finally looked up with a look of defeat, "come inside, and I'll explain," he said in a low voice.

The three men went inside the house. Coming inside again was different than before, both Ryan and Don marveled at the size, and how the house was decorated. It was elegant, but felt homey with a flare of Europe mixed with Latino influence. The front part of the house was striking, and walking into it made you turn your head constantly to see what was on the walls. Ryan felt as if he were a tourist entering a museum, not a house. When they had searched it, they didn't take the time to notice all the different things that were on the walls. Fallon led them to a back part of the home, and sat slowly down in a chair that magnified his small stature. He indicated for Ryan, and Don to sit across from him.

"If either one of you would like something, I can get it for you, what I have to tell you may take some time, it's very uncomfortable for me to admit to, and I haven't told anyone about it. The only people that know about it seem to be ending up dead, so I'm sure you can understand my reluctance. Right now it may be the only way to save my life at this point."

With that he sat, and told the two detectives the entire story. The story of Aubrey's Father, and how he traded different favors for sex with his young daughter, and how each of those men was now being found dead. Each sordid detail sickened the two men, and they took no shame in showing it to Fallon in their faces. Both understood now how this revenge was playing out, and how the men that were pursuing the girl would become victims. Fallon had a right to be concerned about Aubrey, or whoever was taking the law into their own hands.

Don stopped Fallon after a few minutes, and explained that he really needed to consult a lawyer before he went any further.

"The more you tell us, the more you're implicating yourself in a crime," Don told him. "We need to read you your rights, and take you down to the station to finish this interview."

Fallon nodded his head, and looked at the ground, "I'm afraid I'll be next," he said in a low voice.

He looked up at the two detectives, and indicated he needed to use the restroom down the hall. Fallon got up, and went toward the room, disappearing around the corner with the lock of the door.

Ryan watched as Don got up, and got him some water out of the large refrigerator in the kitchen. He took a long drink, and then looked back at Ryan. The two men remained silent until Don broke the stalemate with a long belch.

"Sorry," he said. "Sure is taking him a long time in there, isn't it."

He started down the hallway and tried the knob on the door, it was locked, "Fallon," he said into the blank door. "Fallon, you ok?"

There was no answer on the other side. Ryan had now joined him at his side with his service pistol drawn. The two men stepped back and Don took a good kick at the door. It immediately fell off the hinges to an empty room. The window was open, and Fallon was gone.

"Damn," Don said with aggravation in his voice. "We've got to find that girl; this guy's a ticking bomb."

Chapter Fifteen

Terrible things happen to terrible people, perhaps not as often as they should, but things in the world seem to take care of rotten souls with regularity. Old-aged crooks and thieves seem to be in short supply throughout the world. It was that knowledge that kept her mind on what she was doing as she drove away from the mansion. She had seen the detectives pulling out of the parking lot, and knew she needed to hurry if she was to get done what needed to be done. Fallon was going to fear for his life, it was her intent to make him wonder about what was happening for every second he was awake. Then she would make him dream about it, until he woke up with his conscience constantly thinking about what could happen to him. Her mission was nearly complete, and she needed to make the final two on her list suffer. After they were dealt with, she would go back, and take care of the one that was supposed to be the protector. For now, her intent was to let both remaining men know she knew where they were, and could get to them any time she wanted to.

She had watched the ambulance leave with the body of the fat slob, Massey. She waited just long enough to make sure he was gone, and put away in whatever morgue they would take him to. The sight of him being loaded in the back of the truck made her feel calm; some of the pressure and stress she had felt was lifted. He was one of the worst of the men, and his murder was sweet success to her, a very sweet success.

She switched on the radio, and pushed the button to change stations. She was looking for a news talk show, one that would give the details of the days work. She felt a twinge of regret over the worker in the store, but that soon passed, she knew he was just another man, and right now, she had no use for men.

She looked up just in time to see the red light, and got the car stopped at the same time she found the station she was looking for. The news was already on, and they were just getting to the part about the victims.

"One man dead and another injured," the newsperson said on the air. "The injured man has been identified as Harold Massey, and the dead man's identity is being withheld pending notification of next of kin. Mr. Massey was taken to Baptist Hospital, and is listed in critical condition. The police have no suspects at this time, but are speculating this murder may be connected with the recent string of killings here in the city."

She immediately punched the button on the radio to shut it off. Injured, she thought to herself, how could they say he was injured, she saw him die. Her mind was racing, and the noise in her ears was deafening, she needed to think, but the ringing was getting worse, and she realized she was at the traffic light, and the car behind her was honking while making gestures at to her to get going.

It wasn't in her plan to fail at any of what she thought of as justified killings. She had planned this meticulously with timing that was precise, and the result was deliberate. None of the plan had survival by any of the men. The murders were torturous, and painful, and if one failed, all of them failed.

She pulled her car into a parking lot at what looked like an abandoned building with a huge blue and white faded sign, blasting to the world that the building was "For Sale". A wealthy family had owned the building for years and not many knew that even with the sign, buying the building would be a hard task. Several developers had tried to obtain it for apartments, or lofts. Some claimed it would revitalize the area, and some would tell the truth, and show her how they were going to tear it down, and start anew with everything from museums to shopping malls. She never gave any of them any thought, and knew the owner didn't either.

She walked in on the side, looking around as if to check for someone watching her. She knew there weren't many people in the area at least not any that cared about a well-dressed woman entering an abandoned building. Never the less, she always felt compelled to look around, and make sure there was no one that would follow her inside.

Once she made her way past the dark entrance, she took some stairs to the second floor, and then boarded an old freight elevator. It was noisy, and worn out, but it still worked, and so she kept it in place. The old elevator aided in throwing those that came in uninvited off. Not many would think someone would actually use it to get up to the third floor. To look at the broken wood planks in the floor, and faded paint on the gate, you would never think someone would find the nerve to step into it, let alone ride it.

It lumbered slowly up with the aches and pains of age, creaking in its metal pulleys, and worn ropes. She held on to a well fastened handle that she had installed when she first started living there, hoping if the floor ever did give way, at least she could hang on until the elevator reached it's destination.

When the noise finally stopped, she stepped forward into what some would think was a room out of place. Over the past three years she had worked hard on collecting things she always longed for and could never have. Her design was impeccable in the loft, with spiraling columns that dominated the room. The open space reminded her there were no boundaries that you needed to keep yourself inside, and creativity had become one of the most important things to her. She had decided to leave everything in her old life behind, even Aubrey. She knew that someday she would see her daughter again, but until that happened she would use all her energy to do what she wanted to do. That is until she found out about what was happening to Aubrey. Her obsession to change her life from one of obedience and pain was now channeled in a different direction. With her determination she would right the wrongs, and pull herself together to move forward in the direction that she was going now. It was an easy decision, there was no reluctance involved, but it had been a hard transition to think of her previous life again.

She went immediately into the pantry located just off the kitchen, and retrieved a small glass jar with several vials and hypodermic needles inside. The contents were something she kept secret. She took one needle out, and one small vial with clear liquid inside.

Her thoughts were now on Massey, and the fact the media had reported him being alive, but in critical condition at the hospital. She knew that it was imperative she finished her task before he could improve, and speak with the authorities. It was something she had to do, and it wasn't a desire anymore, it was a necessity, at least in her mind. She put the needle in her purse, and walked to the back of the room.

In front of her was a door to what she liked to think was the room where throw away items would be placed. She freely admitted to being somewhat of a packrat and most everything that had little meaning at all ended up in this room. Right now it had an occupant that she fully intended on throwing away, but not just yet.

The door had a lock on the outside and one on the doorknob as well. She clicked the key into the lock, and then turned the door lock, allowing her to open the door. The open door flooded the small room with light from the rest of the house. Lying in the middle was a man, tied around his ankles, and his wrists, with a rope connecting the two. He had been asleep the last time she looked in, but this time was quite awake. She could see his eyes widen, trying to adjust to the sudden influx of bright light. The blindfold she had placed over his eyes had fallen around his neck. She peered in, purposely standing in the door, creating a shadow figure for him to look at.

She could see he had moved, and one of his shoulders was clearly out of place because of his attempt to loosen the ropes. She stepped forward, and placed her right foot on the separated shoulder. His eyes closed with pain, a pain so sharp it prevented him from uttering anything other than a grunt.

She looked down into his eyes. "Painful?" she asked him. "If you keep moving around, you'll separate the other one, and then you'll know what real pain is."

She backed out of the room, looking at him as she went. Everything here was going well, very well, he was terrified and in pain, and he knew she was holding all the cards. She would work her way to the hospital, and take care of the business that was left undone earlier in the day.

She stopped at the doorway, and looked at him one more time. For a split second she felt a tinge of pity for him, looking at her with a cry for sympathy in his eyes. She could tell he was still in shock over the fact that she was even able to get him to the house and tie him up. He thought she was weak, and now he knew different, all the things he had done to her were about to catch up with him. He was supposed to protect the things he loved, and now the only thing he protected was the beer he poured down his throat every night. That and his precious friends, the ones he thought would carry him through his life with ease. Her pity quickly subsided, with rage and guilt starting to take over again. She took a final look at him and shut the door, slamming the lock closed as she did.

She gathered her composure back as she stood in front of the door; it wasn't hard for her to slip in and out of anger. It was something she had done for many years, now it seemed easier to do. She went to the kitchen and poured herself some water, then brushed back her hair, and headed to the creaky elevator she had arrived in. Her guilt built with every step, she had asked herself many times how she could have let this happen to Aubrey, and happen right under her nose.

She drove the speed limit to the hospital, thinking of the task at hand. There was no urgency in her driving, because she thought she would have some time before Massey regained consciousness. She thought of how he had looked when he was wandering around in the huge warehouse, his face red with anger, and then the realization he was in trouble. His eyes bulged, and she could see how he wondered what was happening to him. She thought it had been a wonderful plan, a plan that would virtually scare him to death. Make him feel the fear, and pain all at one time. She smiled again at the thought.

She pulled into the Baptist Hospital, and put on the white smock she kept with her. She knew it would someday come in handy, and today it looked like her training would pay off. She put the needle in her pocket, and went inside. Inside the lobby, she noticed two or three uniformed policemen as they stood in front of the elevators and another group by the stairs. One more was talking to the elderly lady that manned the information booth at the front. She stepped lively, and with confidence, going past all of them, and pushing the button to go up on the elevator. She didn't know yet where Massey was in the hospital, but she could look at one of the nurse's stations without raising any suspicions, and find him quickly. The door to the elevator opened, and she stepped in, quickly pushing the button for the doors to close. When the door was just starting to close, a hand flew in and stopped it, making the door open one more time. Two men stepped into the elevator. They were both wearing suits and ties, looking very much like the two detectives she had seen earlier in the parking lot. She turned her head toward the elevator wall, and tried to hide her features, she wasn't sure if the men had seen her face earlier at the two crime scenes.

"Please press three for us," the tall one said without looking at her.

She did as she was asked, and then pressed the button for the fourth floor. The elevator moved slowly, and she listened as intently as she could without looking like she was snooping. Both men talked, but talked in a low voice, so she couldn't catch everything they said. The one thing she did get was Massey had just been taken to the third floor after surgery, and they hoped he was awake so they could talk with him.

They exited on the third floor, and turned to the right, walking at a brisk pace down the hallway. She quickly poked her head out, and watched as the two men walked halfway down the hall, then stopped in front of a room. She moved back inside, and went to the fourth floor. She got out, and quickly headed for the stairs at the end of the hall. Along the way she picked up a stack of towels that were lying on a cart, and carried them with her.

When she reached the third floor, she walked normally to the door the two detectives had gone to. Sitting in a chair next to the door was a uniformed officer that stopped her from going in.

"There are some detectives in there right now, can you wait a few minutes before you go in?" he asked.

She started to turn, and walk back to the stairs when the door to the room opened, and the two detectives walked out, "he's still under the anesthetic," Ron told the sitting officer. "Make sure that no one gets in the room except medical personnel; we clear?"

The officer nodded as he stood up, and acknowledged to the two men, he knew they were leaving, and they didn't have anything to worry about. They went back toward the elevator without looking at what seemed to be a nurse standing at the side of the hallway. They disappeared into the elevator quickly, and she turned to go back in the room, and finish her deed.

The officer put up no resistance as she walked by, as if she were supposed to be there. Once inside she put the towels in the bathroom, and went to the bedside of Massey. His huge body took the whole bed, and then some. Tubes were coming from almost every opening and appendage. He was breathing, but it was with the help of a machine. His eyes were closed, and there was the steady beep of the monitor that was attached to his heart. She stood over him for a minute, looking, wondering if he could indeed hear what she would say to him. She had been told even though one is in a coma, the person could still hear, and probably comprehend what was being said to them.

She leaned over close to his ear, "Mr. Massey," she whispered. "I'm sorry I didn't get the job done earlier, I hope you can forgive me."

She took the needle from her pocket, and squirted a tiny bit of the liquid into the air. She flipped her finger a couple of times on the side of the glass tube, and looked for any air to surface to the top. Then she turned and put the needle into the IV sticking out of his arm, and depressed the plunger.

It only took a few seconds for the liquid to act, his face went limp, and the steady beep of the monitor went to a steady tone. He was dead, this time she knew it was finished. The alarm on the monitor sounded, and she put the needle back in her pocket, turned and went to the door. The officer was standing at the sound of the alarm, and several nurses were coming quickly to the room. She turned toward the stairs, walked briskly to the door, and went down toward the lobby once more. She felt a relief again, much like the morning episode. She took the smock off, and left it in the stairway, opened the door, and walked calmly away.

The people in the lobby had no way of knowing what had just happened, the police however got an indication of something on the radio. The officer that was standing at the information booth looked upset at the transmission, and quickly indicated to the other officers in the room to head to the elevator. She kept walking, trying not to draw attention to herself before she could reach the front door. She opened the lobby doors, and went to her car, got in and started to drive away. Baptist Hospital sits directly on the road, just off the Henley Street Bridge. She drove out of the hospital, and started to the corner when she caught the two detectives out of the corner of her eye. They were standing under the cover off to the side discussing something. She quickly gave them a glance, and kept driving. They never knew she was there, at least not yet.

She looked in her rear view mirror, and noticed the two running toward the entrance. They would hurry upstairs, and find Mr. Massey would not recover to speak with them. The uniformed officer would tell them there was a nurse had come in, and left as soon as the alarm sounded, but it didn't matter, she would be long gone by then.

The doctor's would be able to figure out Massey had been killed with the injection, but that too would take time. She felt confident she had some time to get done what she needed to do. Fallon would be her next conquest, and while they tried to determine how he had managed to get himself killed, she would get the one they called, Scooter. She only needed to stay one step ahead, and soon it would all be over.

She turned right onto the Henley Street Bridge, and drove away at the speed limit. It was time to go home and rest for a while. She needed some rest, and then she would check on Aubrey again, just to make sure she was ok, just to make sure the police weren't too close to her yet.

Chapter Sixteen

Aubrey and Amy sat in the bedroom playing a game of UNO, for the first time in what seemed ages. The game had been their favorite when they were little girls, trying to match the colors or numbers, out witting your opponent, and laughing so hard when one or the other came up with a draw four. This game wasn't played with nearly the same amount of joyful laughs as others in the past, but the two were having some fun anyway, in the wake of what was happening.

Amy's Mom was in the kitchen trying to stay calm, and fix all of them something to eat. She had called her sister, and asked if Amy could stay with her this weekend because of Aubrey. She was her usual "I can't understand you" self, and gave her the hard time she expected, but in the end she agreed.

The last few days had been very hard on her, and of course the two girls, but she tried hard to show a positive face to them. Deep inside she thought she could scream out loud sometimes, and privately she felt as if she were living in hell. She felt as if all the murder and carnage was coming down on top of her, she was alone in this. Things of this magnitude always happened to other people, not you. Aubrey needed help, and her daughter was looking to her to give it. She put both her hands on the counter, and leaned hard on her arms. She hung her head, and tired once more not to break out in tears. It took her several minutes, but she managed to get herself together, and then continue on with her daily duties.

She could hear the girls in their room, sometimes letting out a series of hilarious laughter. She could hear them slapping each other on the arms, and rolling in playful fighting on the bed or floor. She thanked God they could forget their problems long enough to escape back into childhood. Sara managed a smile, and wished with all her might she could go up to the room and participate in the childhood game they were playing, but of course she couldn't.

The day had sprung into a bright, sunny beginning, bringing some warmth to the frozen tundra outside. It was still cold, but the weatherman had promised it would be warm enough today to bring some melting to the snow. Sara stared outside into the vast white of snow, and watched as some of the ice melted off of a tree in her backyard, and took its fatal plunge into the yard. She was daydreaming, not of anything in particular, just looking out the window like you did when you were in school. A thousand thoughts pranced through her mind, and not a single one would be remembered.

She was jolted back into reality when Aubrey and Amy burst into the kitchen, both still clad in pajamas. They were still in a childlike state, demanding each other to stop, begging for something to eat. It was hard to believe they were seventeen.

Seventeen she thought, Aubrey was seventeen, and no one had even told the poor girl Happy Birthday. Sara had told herself she wouldn't forget her birthday, but she had.

She turned, and opened her arms for a hug, "Aubrey, I forgot your birthday, Happy Birthday honey," she said in a motherly way.

Aubrey looked at her with a puzzled face, then the realization her birthday had indeed come and gone without even a mention from anyone.

"Wow, I did turn seventeen," she said, and took the hug that Sara offered her.

Amy joined in with them, then suddenly shot back, and ran out of the room, "I got you a present," she yelled as she ran down the hallway.

It was only seconds before she bounded back into the room with a brightly wrapped gift in her hands. It wasn't large, but the wrapping was beautiful, and Amy held it out, offering it to Aubrey as if it were gold. Aubrey stood perfectly still, looking at the present but not reaching for it. She was living a moment she had wished would happen again for years now. Amy pushed the gift toward her with a smile.

"Take it," she prodded. "It's yours, all yours."

Aubrey reached for the box, and pulled in close to her chest. Tears were starting to trickle down her cheeks, and both Sara and Amy noticed she was starting to cry. Neither said a word, they only stood there with smiles on their faces. They knew her family had all but forgotten Aubrey on her birthday, so both helped her savor the moment of getting an unexpected gift.

Finally Aubrey tore the paper from the box, and quickly ripped the tape off of where it held the top together. Inside she found a necklace with only half a heart pendant attached. It was broken as if someone had torn it in two. It was Sterling Silver, and had a silver chain attached. She took it out of the velvet box that held it, and looked with wondering eyes. Then she looked at Amy, who had taken an identical necklace out of her blouse, and held it up for Aubrey to see.

"This means we'll always be friends," Amy said with tears coming to her eyes as well. "We have half of each others heart to wear forever, and as long as we have it, we will be together somehow, some way."

The two hugged each other hard as sisters will do, and Sara joined in on the celebration. After a few seconds of weeping and hugging, Sara leaned back, and told the girls she would fix them something to eat. She went into the kitchen and opened the refrigerator door, looked up and closed it once again.

"I think we need something else to eat," she said. "I think I need to take you two out to the mall, we can eat, and I can get Aubrey a gift also."

"You don't have to do that," Aubrey said.

"Yes she does," Amy interjected. "I think we'll have fun at the mall, let's go get dressed, race you!"

The two girls ran from the room, and Sara let out a satisfied sigh. Maybe they had managed to forget what was going on for the time being. Maybe a trip to the mall, a trip with all of them acting like life was normal again, would indeed help it become that way. She would file the troubles of the past days in the back of her mind, and try to let them sit idly by as she, her daughter and her friend had some fun together.

The two rushed back into the room, flushed with excitement, and ready for whatever the day would bring them as long as it was shopping. Aubrey called shotgun in the car, and the three drove merrily away from the house.

Across the street, Roger Fallon sat in his black Mercedes, waiting until he saw the garage door open, and the car go down the street. He started his car, and followed as he had been planning since the two detectives had visited with him. His objective was to keep this young girl in his sights as long as he could. If she planned on killing, him, she would have to do it in front of everyone, because he had no intention of letting her out of his sight.

He stayed far enough behind that the three women couldn't see him in his car. He didn't worry about them knowing the car; he had traded his BMW for just that reason. Aubrey had seen it before, and he knew she admired it. She had told him once how pretty she thought it was, and how she hoped she could have one when she got old enough to drive. He took it as a hint that maybe she wanted him to buy it for her, but doing that would be impossible to hide, so he shrugged it off as just a young girl being complimentary of her man's automobile.

It took about fifteen minutes for the three women to pull into the mall parking lot. They drove around until they found a close enough parking space, and as soon as the car was stopped, Amy and Aubrey jumped out, and almost ran into the bank of doors welcoming all the customer's money they could handle.

Fallon parked his car not far away, and slowly got out staying within eyeshot of the girls. Amy's mother was lagging behind when they got out of the car, but reached the door not far behind them. He could see they got together not too far inside the building as they stopped by the huge map of the floor plan, looking for the store they thought they could get the most out of the quickest. Fallon followed as they went into the first store around the corner, and disappeared in the sea of material and bright colors of a women's shop. He waited patiently outside the store for a few minutes, and the three returned for the trip down the busy mall corridor to the next venture.

Aubrey, didn't have any money, and looked at Sara with pitiful eyes, begging for something to help her get through the next few days.

"A new outfit will do me good," she pleaded in her best little girl voice. "When I get back to my house, I can get your money back, I promise."

Sara looked at her, and started to lose her resolve not to spend too much money. She had intended to buy Aubrey a birthday gift, but she was asking for almost one hundred dollars to spice up her wardrobe. Sara wasn't sure she could swing that kind of money for a present for a non-family member. Aubrey was standing in front of her with pleading eyes, and her hands were folded in a prayer like manner. Amy was standing back holding back a hysterical laugh that was welling up inside her.

"Ok, ok," Sara finally succumbed to the request. "Listen though, I had planned on buying you a gift, but that was only fifty dollars, you have to pay me back the other fifty, understood?"

Aubrey listened intently to Sara as she spelled out the terms to her agreement. While Sara was talking, Aubrey let her eyes wander around the mall fronts, unconsciously looking into the windows of the stores. When her eyes passed the huge front windows of a popular sports apparel store, she noticed the reflection of what looked like someone she knew.

Sara and Amy both noticed the change in Aubrey's facial expression at the same time.

"What's the matter, Aubrey?" both asked simultaneously.

All the color left her face, and her eyes started shooting around the room as if she were looking for some place to run and hide. Sara looked at her, and then took her arm. She started leading her down the corridor where she might feel safer.

"Whatever it is, it won't hurt you, Aubrey, we're here with you and we'll help, no matter what."

Aubrey just kept her head down, watching the floor pass by as they walked. Her mind was racing, and she was starting to feel light headed, she knew she would pass out if she didn't sit down, and do it quick. She tried to pull Sara over to the benches in the center of the mall. Both women slipped just a little, but Amy caught her arm, then the three went to the middle. Aubrey sat with Sara kneeling in front of her, and Amy beside her.

"What was it, Aubrey?" Sara insisted.

Aubrey looked around one more time; this time she didn't see the man she thought she knew. Maybe it was her imagination, and her eyes were just playing tricks on her. She sat up straight trying to get a better view of the people that were walking by, some staring now at what looked like a young girl about to faint.

"I guess it's nothing," she finally said to Sara. "I just thought I saw someone, but it must have been a mistake, that's all, a mistake."

Sara looked around the mall too, searching for an unknown person she wouldn't know if they walked up and said hello. Whatever it was that upset Aubrey, it had happened quick, and whoever did it, knew it, and probably disappeared as quick as they came, "lets go to the food court, and get you something to drink," she told the two girls.

Roger Fallon came back from beside the plant where he had hid quickly when Aubrey spotted him. The women started walking toward the center of the mall again, this time he kept a longer distance. He felt in his pocket for the gun he had placed there before he left his house, and moved it slightly just to make sure it was still in place. He had to wait until the three were clear of others before he put his plan into play, so he decided he would keep a larger distance behind them for a short time.

They were starting to walk faster, and he could see they were gathering up the playful mood they were in a few minutes ago. They turned, and went into the food court, immediately walked over to the *Dairy Queen*, standing in line patiently until they were waited on.

The food court wasn't crowded, only a few stragglers were cutting through or sitting with one another, resting their tired feet from the constant walking a mall demands. In front of Fallon was a hat kiosk, loaded with sports hats, funny sayings, and hats of every color imaginable. He stood behind it watching intently to see if and where the three would go to sit. The young man that was on duty trying to sell hats for a living, came around, and asked him if he could help. Fallon ignored him, and moved around the side of the kiosk, dismissing the request as if it had never been offered. The young man pursued him, and finally Fallon decided a hat might be helpful after all. He pulled out a twenty, and gave it to the boy, grabbed a black hat with some saying about how great a Dad he was, and crunched it down on his head. Then he moved to the edge of the food court with his hand in his pocket, his fingers circling the pistol. He moved around the perimeter of the food court, looking for the right spot to take care of his problem. If she was going to try to kill him, he was going to do it first.

He stopped by a large column, and leaned against it. He had never killed anyone, but the events of the last couple of days required drastic actions, and it was his intent to take care of this quickly. His only fear was the panic he felt creeping up inside his head; it was something he had fought since he decided to remove the threat for himself. The police didn't seem to want anything to do with it; they scoffed at his demand for help.

He looked around the column, and tried to focus on which table the three women were sitting at. Again, Fallon ducked back behind to his hiding place. He touched the gun one more time, this time keeping his hand on it. He would have to move quickly, so he decided he would walk toward them, pull the gun out, and start firing. He was a pretty fair shot; at least he thought he was. Sweat dripped from his brow onto his free hand. The liquid startled him so he stayed put for a moment, trying to gather his composure once more.

Across from him, detectives, Ryan Rose, and Don Breeding entered the food court. They too had followed the three women, though it wasn't for the same reason. Both wanted to talk with Aubrey one more time before an arrest was made by an over zealous media group. Ryan had eliminated Aubrey in his mind. Don wasn't as quick to make that determination though. He thought she was involved in some way, she may not be the actual killer, but she knew more than she was telling.

It took a few seconds for them to spot the women sitting in the middle of the court smiling, and happily eating ice cream. They started across the room toward them when Fallon came out from behind the column. Don was the first to notice the little man running toward the Aubrey. In his hand was a gun, he wasn't shooting yet, but Don saw it, and reacted immediately.

"Gun!" he yelled as he pulled his from its holster. He stopped, and steadied himself as the first shot was fired from Fallon's pistol. A young man standing one table over from the women went down in a scream of pain. The noise from the pistol, and the scream from the young man were followed with several screams, and people started to run in every direction. Ryan fired at the same time as Don, and Fallon went backwards in an uncontrollable fall. His gun went off again, and part of the ceiling fell down on two customers. Both detectives stood like statues waiting to see if he got up again. He didn't move.

Aubrey and Amy were under the table with Sara on top of them. They had ducked as soon as they heard the first shot and heard the scream. Aubrey's hands were over her ears, but she could hear herself screaming above everything. She looked out from under the table, and saw Fallon stretched out on his back, blood running from his chest and his head. She thought she had seen him when they were in the mall corridor, but had dismissed it as her imagination. Sara got off of the two girls, and stood back by the table they were sitting at.

"You can get up girls," Detective Rose said to them. "It's over now, you're safe.

It was the first time that Aubrey thought about it, but it was true, he had been shooting at her. Fallon wanted to kill her. She tried to hold in the terror of such a thought, but her tears started flowing, and she was doing everything not to just get up and run right then.

Amy reached down, and tried to help her up from under the table. Aubrey didn't even realize that Amy had gotten up from under the sanctuary of wood and metal.

She reached for her hand and got up. She saw the mayhem from the shooting. People were standing at the edge of the tables, with Mother's holding their children close, others were hugging each other with the enthusiasm of survival. You could hear the sobs from scared parents, and the teenagers that frequent the mall scene. Employees of the fast food restaurants were starting to come out from under the counters and surveying what had happened.

Ryan walked over to Fallon, and kicked the revolver away from the dead man. Don bent down, and picked it up. Both men were accurate with their shots. Both with deadly aim, two shots fired, and both had hit their target. Ryan took off his jacket, and covered Fallon's head and chest. Mall security had come running when they heard the screams, and were now standing next to the two detectives. Other police officers were starting to arrive on the scene. One approached Ryan with his gun drawn, holding it at Fallon.

"Not necessary," Ryan told him. "Call a bus in here will you, get him out of here as soon as possible."

Don walked up to Aubrey and Amy, and stood directly in front of her, "are you ready to help us figure this out now, Miss Hendrickson?"

Aubrey lowered her head and nodded slowly, "Sara and Amy need to come too," she said. "They need to be there for all of it too."

Don took the young girl by the arm, and started to walk toward the mall entrance at the end of the food court. Sara followed close behind with Ryan at her side. The noise was starting to subside now, and the police had the situation well in hand. The group needed to go to the station, and find out the whole story behind this attempt. They reached the door, and Ryan turned back around just in time to see her, the nicely dressed lady that they had looked for over the past few days. She was standing at the far end of the food court, and when Ryan saw her she flashed a smile, turned and was gone, lost in the sea of people that had come to the food court to see what was happening.

Chapter Seventeen

Ben Hendrickson woke up from a deep sleep. He was dreaming, a dream where he was free again, sitting in his living room having a beer, and watching his favorite television show. He didn't have a worry in the world, and his arms and legs had stopped hurting. He could feel his feet and hands as he lifted the beer from the table next to him. His feeling of freedom was interrupted in his dream by a figure coming in the room, and grabbing him. The figure threw him against the wall, and he fell to the floor. Then the figure came to him, stood over the top of him, with a horrible look on her face. She was screaming at the top of her lungs. The noise caused him to awake, and he realized he was tied up in the dark room again.

He tried in vain for the thousandth time to move his arms and legs. He could no longer feel either his hands or feet, and one of his legs was going numb. The pain in his shoulders subsided hours ago, which allowed him to sleep for a short time, but now it was coming back with a vengeance. He knew if he didn't get out of this soon, he would die in this dark room where no one would ever find him. He wasn't quite sure anyone wanted to find him anyway. He didn't know who had taken him; he was sure it was a woman, but every time she came in, he was either passed out, or so far out of it he couldn't tell anything from her voice. It was far too dark to see, and when she opened the door, the light rushed in, and took him to blindness. It was a bleak situation.

He wasn't sure how long he had been here, but it felt like days, or weeks, he wasn't sure anymore. He saw no light, and felt no heat, his mind was quickly leaving the capacity for reason behind. Hunger plagued him, he knew that, and thirst was beyond a want, he felt he needed water soon or he would parish from dehydration. He tried hard not to slip back into unconscious sleep again. He wanted to be awake when whoever had him, came back this time. He needed to see or hear who they were, and why they wanted to kidnap him. He had no money, or access to get any. His home was modest, and he didn't think he held any secrets so bad they would justify this kind of treatment. The whole matter really had him baffled, so he wasn't sure what to do.

He fought the sleep again, but his eyelids were getting heavy again. The one thing sleep did provide was a break from the constant pain. He would also forget about the hunger and thirst. It was futile to resist, he finally closed his eyes, and drifted back to his dreamland, he realized it was no longer sleep; it was passing out. It didn't matter that he tried to stay awake. His body wouldn't let him. He passed out again.

Just as he was passing into the darkness of sleep, she came in the door from the elevator. Her job seemed to be getting easier all the time. With Fallon she knew his stupidity would take him right to Aubrey, and the note she left on his door would drive him there. She didn't want to risk Aubrey getting hurt, but she was going to be there to stop that. Fortunately she didn't have to, the two detectives wanted to talk with Aubrey, so they took care of the little man that thought he was bigger than he was. They killed him for her, so she could mark him off the list.

The only one left was the one they called Scooter. He was the newest of the scum, only working Aubrey for the last year or so. She felt as if he was truly one that may not want to do what he was doing, he only took Aubrey out of guilt from the other men. She honestly thought maybe Fallon or Massey was blackmailing him into the acts. Regardless, he was going to meet the same fate as the others, one way or another. His motives really didn't matter to her; it was his actions that made her act on her feelings.

She walked aimlessly around the apartment thinking of all the happenings of the past few days. Her feelings were strong, but for some reason she felt alone, and it was really hard to remember things from weeks ago, and almost impossible from years ago. She worried about it, but didn't let her keep from the focus of Aubrey.

She heard her unwilling guest move in the room where she kept him from escaping. Perhaps it would be wise to give him some food or water after all. The slow death of starvation and dehydration really wasn't her idea of the way he should die. Preventing him from eating obviously got his attention, so maybe it was time to give him something to keep him going, until it was time for her real plan for him to come true. She went to the kitchen, and filled a bowl with water, and then she opened the locked door, and entered with the flood of light coming with her. He moved slightly, but she could see he was having trouble opening his eyes. The combination of being in the dark, and the light sifting through the darkness, kept him from seeing clearly. She didn't speak because she was afraid he might recognize her voice, so she laid the water next to his head, and touched his shoulder, stood up, and turned to walk back out. She closed the door behind her, and stepped back into the kitchen to make some soup for him to feast on.

Ben could feel the bowl at his lips, and stuck his tongue into the water. It was cool, and felt great on his tongue. He sipped, and was able to get a small amount down his throat. It cooled his inside all the way down, and he could feel it travel all the way down. He lapped the water like a dog, and soon it was too far down in the bowl for him to reach. He accidentally tipped the bowl over, and the remainder of the water spilled onto the floor. He felt desperation fill his body as the water slipped under his cheek, mocking his thirst as if to say, here I am, but you can't have me.

He tried to lap it up from the cold floor with no luck. It was gone, and he was back to not having the wonderful liquid available again. The bowl was upside down on the floor in front of his face, so he picked his head up, and tried to move it behind him. He slipped the bowl with his cheek, and neck, sliding it under him, and simply moved his body around it. It was now sitting at the back of his head.

He wiggled upward a short distance, and became extremely tired with that little movement. He rested for a short time until he caught his breath, and started to wiggle upward again. The bowl was now at the mid part of his back. His arms and shoulders were shooting pain throughout his whole body, but he was determined to get the bowl even with his hands. He wiggled a few more inches, and had to stop again, waiting for his energy to build once more. He kept his eyes closed, and listened more than he watched for his captor to come back to the door. He couldn't hear anything out in the other room; there was only silence.

He scooted on the floor one more time, and felt the cool glass on his fingertips. He grasped the bowl with what little strength he had, and tried to slam it against the floor. Nothing happened; the bowl remained in its original shape. Then he tried again, and got the same result. Again he stopped, waiting for the pain in his arms to subside.

She searched the cupboards for soup or anything liquid he could eat easily without having to be untied. After a few minutes she gave up, and went back to the living area. She stopped when she thought she heard a noise coming from the room, and turned her head to listen. She heard nothing, so she grabbed her coat, and started toward the elevator door. She would have to go out, and get him something. It was late but the convenience store was close, so she would walk down and buy a couple of cans of soup. A little something to eat, just enough it would sustain life in his limp body and keep him going for a few more days. Again, she thought she heard a noise come from the room, this time much louder, and with more force. She stopped, and again her hesitation was met with silence. She worked the rickety elevator door down, and started her descent to the bottom floor.

Ben stopped after the second hit on the floor, and waited. The delay was, as much for him to regain strength, as it was to make sure his subjugator wouldn't here the noise he was making. He tried once more, and at last, felt part of the bowl breaking away, falling to the floor. He dropped the biggest part of the bowl, and felt for the piece that broke off. Once he found it, he started to rub it on the rope that bound his hands, back a forth in a sawing motion. He had to stop again to regain strength, but now some of his adrenalin was helping him, so he started sawing quickly again. After only a few minutes he felt the rope move, then it snapped; plunging his feet away from his body causing him to straighten up immediately. The pain consumed his body, and he felt dizzy as his legs fell limp to the floor. His hands were still bound, but it didn't take long to get through the rope, and both of his hands fell free. His shoulder shot pain through him as if he was stabbed, and that arm became useless for anything other than hanging there.

He was on his side now, with the majority of the ropes cut through, and hanging from his ankles, and wrists. He tried to move his legs, but they only moved slightly with a great deal of pain. Slowly he moved them back and forth, until he could start feeling them again. When the blood started flowing through his limbs again, some of the throbbing slipped away. He was beginning to feel again, not only in his legs, but his arms, and wrists too. He continued to move his feet, and legs, now in a bicycle movement against the floor. Finally he decided it was time to try to move into a sitting position, and see if he could put any weight on the rest of his body. He put his arm down, and pushed upward, first to his elbow and then upright. The maneuver was almost like a victory in sports; he was elated at what he accomplished. Not only was he able to sit, he was able to do it without making any noise at all. He felt a smile come on his face as he sat alone in the dark room. Suddenly he felt like a little child when he took his first steps. His other arm was throbbing with pain. He knew he had a separated shoulder, but until he was able to free himself from this prison, he would have to put up with it.

Ben sat still for several minutes, thinking of things as they used to be. He told himself that after this ordeal, he would have to make amends with Aubrey, and start his life over with some dignity. He bowed his head in shame, and tears started to fall. He had lost everything, his wife, his daughter and now he nearly lost his life. His shame was tremendous so he told himself; no he prayed he could change all of it. Perhaps he could become what he wanted to be; maybe he could work his way back to being a father, and someday be a husband again.

It was time for him to stand on his own, both figuratively, and literally. He tried to push himself up from the floor, and move to the door. He knew his captor locked it, but he would try anything to get free. Perhaps he could break the door down, or work the lock loose somehow, he wasn't sure; he just knew he now had to try.

He finally made it to his feet with great pain, and little wobbles. He ran into a wall with shelves attached to it. Some things fell to the floor with noise he was sure would have gotten the attention of whoever was holding him. There was nothing from outside the door. He felt some excitement as he realized maybe she wasn't there at the moment, maybe she had left after giving him the water. He tried to walk again, and made one step, and then two. Those turned into two more, and he reached the door. He had to lean on the door for a few moments as he caught his breath, and tried to gather his strength once more. If he couldn't walk four steps without almost collapsing from exhaustion, how could he break a door down, or even get out to the street. He took a deep breath, and tried the door in hopes it wasn't locked. To his surprise it opened, and the light came crashing in. He hid his eyes with his good arm, and tried to get his bearings. He had been in the dark for so long it took minutes for him to get adjusted to the light.

He was in a large room, a loft that was decorated, and bright. It held the appearance of someone that was proud of the home they had made. There were big windows, and openness. Along side the room was a spacious kitchen with some food, and drinks setting on the counter. He went to the side of the counter, and leaned on it heavily. He grabbed whatever was in front of him, and shoved it into his mouth. There were potato chips, and some pieces of bread that tasted as if it were part of his first meal. He took huge gulps of water, reaching for the faucet when the glass was empty, and refilling it several times. He turned back around, and realized it was time to abandon the food and drink, and attempt to flee. He surveyed the room, but saw no door, only a hole in the wall where an elevator was supposed to be sitting. It wasn't there, and his hopes for escape started to fade. He had come too far to give up, besides he had made the promise for a new life, and in that new life, there was no giving up.

He looked down the hole where the elevator was supposed to be. At the bottom he could see the top of the car; it was an open car with no ceiling. On the floor he could see the wood was rotted and some was missing. He looked up the shaft to see if there was anything that could aid his flight from this nightmare. Only the ropes that held the dilapidated elevator hung with ominous frailty, far too gone it seemed to hold anything. If it still held the elevator up, a few more pounds wouldn't make it fall, he thought. He decided the only way out was to jump, and climb down the rope to the bottom of the shaft, and go out from there. He was still weak from the lack of food and water, but he had decided he was going to do this, and do it he would. He had nothing to lose; if he missed he would fall, and probably be killed. If he stayed, his captor would surely return, and he would befall the same fate. Only a few feet separated him from freedom, the freedom to go to the police, and report what had happened to him, then find Aubrey, and start this life over. That is if she could ever forgive him. His miserable existence was finally starting to make some sense.

Ben steadied himself against the wall. The pain in his arm was enormous. He supposed if the shoulder was separated, it would surly break when he hit the rope. He looked at the distance one more time, trying to calculate in his mind how far, and how hard he would have to launch his frail body. Only a couple of feet, he told himself, only a couple of feet to jump to freedom. He leaned on the wall and thought he would use his body to help initiate his jump. He pushed off with his legs, and at the same time reached for the rope with his good arm. He felt it hit his palm, gripping it as hard as he could. He slipped a few inches, but his hand connected, and he stopped a few inches down the rope. Ben opened his eyes, and saw he was hanging with one arm on the rope, and both of his legs wrapped around it in a tight grip. After a few moments he started to lower his body down until he was precariously standing on the rotten wood floor of the elevator.

He was so happy he almost started to cry with joy. He turned around slowly, and realized he was in a small hallway that led down a small flight of stairs. At the bottom, there was a door with no window in it. He could see the light under it so he started down, hoping it was the way to the outside world. His only hope was to get outside, and walk until he could flag down a policeman, he had no money, and he didn't know where he was in the city, or if he was even still in Knoxville. The stairs were old, and creaky, and felt soft under his step. This building was obviously not taken care of as the apartment he had just left. Graffiti adorned the walls, and the door had no paint on it. The handrail had been broken off the wall long ago, with pieces of it still hanging on to the anchors with dear life. His arm was killing him, and he really needed to lean on the wall and rest, but inside he was afraid he might go through these walls, and fall to an area where he couldn't get out again. He slowly went down the stairs to the door in front of him.

The outside air was stiff with cold that bit his face with fierce nips of ice. He stopped for a minute to regain the strength in his legs, as the cold seemed to take everything inside him, out. His eyes closed, and he took his hands automatically to his lips, blowing hot air into them to keep from going to what he thought would become frostbite. He turned to the left, and started to walk up the street in the direction of a traffic light he could see at the corner. His walk was weak, but with every step he had a newfound energy to make it to the end of the street and find help. One step, two steps, and then three more. He was finally at the end of the street looking at lights. There were some other people that seemed to be floating aimlessly from one spot to another. He tried to yell, but found himself opening his mouth with nothing coming out. He tried again, and as was the first try, nothing. His head was starting to spin, and he was getting dizzy, he attempted to take another step, and his feet went out from under him. He could feel his body falling in what seemed like slow motion to the ground, his knees hit the sidewalk, and his eyes went black again, as he leapt into unconsciousness one more time.

Ben was sprawled on the sidewalk, half of his body over the curb. He was there only a few minutes when someone noticed him, and came over to see what was going on. The man had no medical training, and frankly, thought he found a homeless drunk out for another day of avoiding reality. He tried to take a pulse on Ben's wrist, a procedure he had seen on television. He couldn't feel anything, but wasn't entirely sure he was doing it right. The man tried another area on Ben's neck, and got the same result, so he took out his cell phone, and dialed 911. He gave the operator the location, and settled in to wait for the help to arrive. He took his jacket off, and put it under the unconscious Ben, then looked around as if he were searching for answers to questions no one was asking. He dove into the man's pocket, and fished out two items, one was a picture of the man and a young girl, his name and the girl's name printed neatly on the back. The other item was a business card for a Detective Ryan Rose. His number printed in raised letters to the police station, and a cell phone number scribbled under the detective's name.

After a few minutes, the police and an ambulance arrived, picked the man up, and whisked him away to the hospital. The police asked the man no questions, and there was no heraldry about what had happened, just a phone call, an ambulance, and he was on his way home to his wife and children.

When he turned to go back to his car he bumped into a nicely dressed woman walking with a few bags in her hands. He excused himself with a smile, and the woman returned the gesture. He continued walking, and she went on her way, back to her apartment to attend to the duties he knew nothing about. The meeting was innocent enough, but he had no idea he had just put into action the demise of one of Knoxville's most notorious killers.

"Just another deed in the day of a good Samaritan," he whispered to himself. "Just another day."

She shook off the small inconvenience of someone running into her in the convenience store isle as she passed, and at the same time she pondered when she saw the ambulance pass in front of the store. She walked with no haste of alarm only that of someone out for the afternoon's essential shopping. There was no need to hurry, she had even stopped and read the headlines of some of the preposterous tabloids at the checkout, "*Jesus returns as an alien*" and "*Woman found with a Buffalo head,*" scribbled in bold print on the front of the paper. The headlines made her chuckle out loud, but her interest wasn't peaked enough to buy the trash she saw in front of her. She looked around the store for a few more minutes, and then bought her wares, and slowly walked back to the loft.

When she came to the door, she noticed it was open, something that was very unusual for her building. She thought she had removed all the unwanted pests from the building, and discouraged others from trespassing with frequent calls to the police when unwanted strangers hung around.

Slowly she slid the door the rest of the way, opening the dark gap to the upstairs. She noticed the door to the elevator was also open, but the lift was still in the position she left it. Hurriedly she went and got up to her floor, and immediately saw the room where she had left her guest was open, and empty. Panic weaved itself through her body until it found the anger hiding inside, and unleashed itself into a horrific scream. A scream she was sure everyone in the neighborhood heard.

Most screams in the night go unnoticed and so did this one, so it disappeared into the emptiness of disconnected concern, just as it had come. She stood paralyzed for several minutes, not knowing what she would, or could do next. She lowered her head, and pondered her overwhelming feeling of defeat. She couldn't succumb to the desire to give up and run, she had come too far, and done far too many things to let this all go so easily. Aubrey was probably safe now, but until the final chess piece had fallen, there is no checkmate. Her guilt kept her in place, thinking, wondering what to do next now that her plans were destroyed.

Chapter Eighteen

Being a detective in any city is a profession that brings you in contact with the worst of the human race. Homicide, vices, and drugs were normal words many on the force used daily, and sometimes hourly. In his years as a policeman, and as a detective, Ryan had not listened to anyone explain the horrible acts that Aubrey told him and Don earlier in the day. He now sat alone in his car, ready to go into his house, play with his small son, kiss the love of his life, and pretend the world was left behind at the station. This night would be a long one, a night of despair, and thoughts that he didn't want to, no, couldn't leave behind. He knew sleep was something that wouldn't come easy tonight, if it came at all.

Aubrey had been in front of them at a table, slowly fidgeting with a pencil while she tried to work up the courage to tell the world all of her secrets. She had tears running down her cheeks, but insisted that what she had to say would come out eventually. This was a promise that she kept, much to the dismay of everyone present. Her recollection of the past few years with her father had riveted everyone in the room to her every word. Each revelation horrified each of them the further she brought them into the reality of deviate behavior. It was something that Ryan would relive over, and over again for years to come.

Her father had virtually "pimped" her out to his friends, not always for money, but for small things, like a ride home from work, or a twelve pack of beer. Sometimes it was because he was drunk, and appreciated someone to talk to, or because he felt Aubrey was the cause of his loneliness. She told of Dr. Cranston, and Bobby Minor, deciding one night that a threesome was in order, and Mr. Williams' constant visits to satisfy desires that his wife wouldn't. Massey was one of the worst, forcing her to do things to his huge body that most prostitutes would refuse; even for three times the amount he gave her slime ball of a father. Her distaste for each of the victims became more and more evident, as she told her horrible stories. Her tone changed with each account, first as a young girl afraid to speak with the detectives, and eventually as a young woman that was angry, and completely full of hate. She eventually ended the tales sounding like a woman with determination and spite.

It amazed Ryan, that Aubrey could speak about the things she had been forced to do, but she became a vessel of her own will, spilling more and more onto the table, until her conscious being was free of the chains that bound her memory. She had been reluctant to start, but once the session was underway, she let herself go, go until all of it was out, and her body was cleansed of the secrets she kept so close to her heart.

The one she hated most was Scooter Sampson. He was the youngest of the men, and the worst for treating Aubrey like she was trash. He made her do things that tore her up inside, and now he was the only one left alive. Ryan knew they needed to find him, and protect him from the worst serial killer Knoxville had ever seen. Part of all of them listening wanted the killer to find him, take care of the business at hand. When Scooter was dead, and all of this was finished, both Ryan and Don were convinced this string of murders would be over.

Her friend Amy, and her mother were present, and the revelations seemed to even surprise them. Aubrey had told both Don and Ryan she had revealed what her father had done to her friends, but none of the details had ever been divulged. To say the two women were shocked would be an understatement, and the irony of that understatement would probably live with the two forever. When Aubrey was telling one of the more detailed meetings, Amy's Mother had gotten up sobbing, excusing herself from the room to go outside. Everyone could hear her wails from inside the room, even Aubrey. The emotional outburst brought Aubrey to a close for a short time, she genuinely felt bad for making someone cry. For a few moments it looked as though the recollection of events was coming to a close, but soon Aubrey started again, telling of the horrible things that had happened to her over the past few years. She finished her tales with the revelation of sanity through her schoolwork.

One of the things Ryan wondered about was Aubrey's Mother in all of this. He found it hard to believe a woman could just walk away from her daughter, especially since Aubrey had told them about her promise to return. Like most good partners, Don had the same thoughts, and brought it up to Aubrey when she took a short break.

"What happened to your mother, Aubrey?" he asked her.

"I've never heard from her, she doesn't call or anything. I thought she couldn't stand the sight of my father or me, so she just left us without saying where she was going."

If anyone had a motive for all of these murders, it was Aubrey, but she insisted she had nothing to do with any of it. She was even more adamant that she didn't know where her father was. It was something Don, and Ryan, believed, as well as the psychologist that was present for the interview. There was no evidence she was telling the truth, or that she was lying, and her alibis were weak, but possible. When she sat down, and opened her soul the way she had to them, it gave both men an instinctive gut feeling that she was telling the truth. Many detectives live on the fact that instinct will get them further than many facts that are given. Ryan wasn't one of those. He believed in the facts, and thought that if you're given all the evidence; the situation will play out to the end. This, however, was a time he had to go on his gut, as did Don.

Suddenly his blind stare into the darkness was interrupted by a loud ring, which startled Ryan back into reality. The inside of the car lit up with the incandescent brightness of the LED on the phone. Ryan reached quickly for the phone, knocking it to the floor. After fumbling around on the floor mat, he finally grasped it and flipped it open, "Detective Rose," was all he said.

An excited voice on the other end started, "my name is Ron, I was walking down the street and found a man unconscious, he had your card in his pocket, and so after I called 911, I called you."

"Please sir, slow down a little bit, you say you found a man on the street, and he had my card in his pocket?"

"Yes, the ambulance has already taken him to the hospital, but I thought if he was carrying a detective's business card around, maybe it was important to let you know."

"Do you know what the man's name is; did he have any identification on him?" Ryan asked.

"Only a picture with him and a young girl in it, on the back it had what looked like his name, and that of the girl, Ben and Aubrey, was written on the back. Does that help at all?"

Ryan thought for a moment, trying to comprehend that this man was telling him he had just found Ben Hendrickson passed out on the road. All the searching, and pleas for help from the public on the television and radio had seemed to go unnoticed, but this man actually did something that would help, without even knowing it.

"Was the man ok?" he asked.

"I don't know," replied the stranger. "They took him to the UT Medical Center; I was just on my way home when I saw him laying there. He looked hurt, and pretty dirty, like he had been in some dirty field for a few days. Other than that, they wouldn't tell me anything. The police were here, but no one talked to me, they just took him away, and I went on my way."

"You've helped a great deal sir, thank you for calling me," Ryan got the man's phone number, and flipped his phone shut.

He looked up at his house, and thought for a moment that he would go inside, only for a short time, and then head to the hospital to see if Ben Hendrickson could tell them anything. It was a fleeting thought. Ryan knew his wife's mood would not be the best, after all he had just cost them their vacation, and it was all for work, a word that caused many disagreements in his household. He started the car, and drove away without letting his wife know he was even there. The entire day had been one of sadness and despair, why change it now, he thought to himself. Laura watched from the living room window as his car disappeared into the darkness. She turned, and attended to their small son with a tear trickling a small trail down her cheek. The tear wasn't from anger, it was for the dedication that her husband showed to his profession, a tear for these victims.

Chapter Nineteen

Sickness sat in the depths of Ryan's insides; he dreaded the thought of talking to Ben Hendrickson. His distaste for the type of man he was, and the ghastly deeds he had set upon his own daughter made it difficult to keep an open mind. Ryan wanted to understand, but these types of crimes were incomprehensible to him. Don was to meet him at the hospital, and Ryan knew that part of his job tonight was to keep him from yielding a heavy hand on Hendrickson. It was something both wanted to do, but they knew it was something the office would not condone, and the cons firmly outweighed the pros.

The two arrived almost simultaneously at the front of UT Medical Center. There were several police cars in front of the lobby as well as plenty of press mingling around waiting to pounce on the first person that looked as though they had answers to questions. Ryan noticed his friend from the largest paper in town, and quickly went over to him. He pulled him aside with a slight tug on his arm and the two went to the side of Ryan's car.

"What have you got for me, Chuck?" Ryan asked him

"Not much really, I found the guy that called you; he was just some poor sap walking along the street when he saw Hendrickson lying there. He was pretty upset, so I believe his story. No one else saw anything, but I did some checking around the neighborhood, and a man said he thought one of the people renting a loft apartment was also named Hendrickson, he didn't know the address though."

Ryan's head popped up, and looked at the reporter, "an address with Hendrickson in the same neighborhood that they found Ben? That has to be more than just a coincidence don't you think?"

The reporter nodded, "you have anything for me, you know, tit for tat?"

"We're going to interview Hendrickson in connection with selling his daughter to the victims, I can't go into much else, but that should help your story just a little."

Ryan patted the reporter on the back, and turned to go back to Don. The remainder of the press had noticed them at the same time, and turned to get whatever statement they had on the matter. Ryan put his finger up to his mouth indicating to Don to stay hush-hush, on the matter.

They walked into the hospital lobby with the rush of questions being hurled at them from both the newspaper reporters and television commentators. Neither detective said anything; they just kept walking to the elevator. Once inside Ryan looked at Don, and took out his notebook, scribbling a name on a small sheet of paper; he handed it to Don.

"Call this guy at the County Recorder, and see if he has any loft apartments registered to the name Hendrickson in the area where Ben was found."

The elevator opened, and both men walked out into the hallway of the Intensive Care Unit. Ryan knew the nurses would stop them from seeing Hendrickson, but you never received anything unless you asked. Ryan had every intention of asking with as much influence as he could muster. If he was awake, Ryan wanted to talk with him. He stopped by the officer in front of the door.

"Are you assigned here all night?" he asked him.

"Yes sir," the officer replied

"I don't want anyone that doesn't have a badge to enter here. You look at every hospital identification, and match it with the face," he looked at him with intentional resolve, "this is important; is it clear?"

Don tapped Ryan on the shoulder, "give him a break Ryan, he understands."

They walked into the ICU, and were immediately met by a gruff looking nurse. She looked as though she had been there since the hospital was opened. She was one of the few nurses that still wore the white shoes and uniform, and hat to match. Her hair was gray, and up the way they wore it in the sixties. She walked with her arms out as if she were expecting a fight at any minute, "what do you want?" she said with authority.

Both men showed their badges at the same time, "don't care if you're the cops from hell, what are you doing in my ICU?" Her voice was even gruffer the second time around, and she looked at them like they were aliens. She didn't stick around for an answer. She turned her back, and walked away with a huff and the wave of her hand.

Ryan got a grin on his face, this was his kind of nurse, she obviously didn't take anything from anybody, "we need to talk to Ben Hendrickson, and I promise we won't be long."

She turned back around, and stared the two men down, "even if he was awake, I wouldn't let you talk to him, you have to wait just like the woman detective that was here a few minutes ago, understand?"

"Wait," Ryan said. "You say there was a woman detective here a few minutes ago?"

"Yea, but her badge was different, some kind of government badge, now scat you two; I have work to do."

"One more question, what did she look like?" Don asked.

"Pretty woman, well dressed, taller than me, but shorter than you, brown hair, short with blond streaks in it, looked real fake, if you know what I mean. Said she'd be back in the morning."

With that she grabbed both arms of the detectives, and showed them the way out the door. They stood beside each other with a gap that was left by the nurse between them. Ryan turned to the officer that was standing diligently by the ICU door.

"Did you check the badge of the woman detective who came in here?" he asked.

The officer looked a little perplexed, "no woman came to this door, and I haven't let anyone in here except you two."

"Is there another way into the ICU?" Don asked with uncertainty.

"Only through the operating room as I understand it," he answered.

Ryan looked at Don, and started to say something, but he interrupted him, "I'm on it, I'll get someone on the other door."

Ryan watched as Don walked away down the hallway to the nurse's station. Both of them were exhausted, and it seemed like there would be no end to the night. They couldn't talk to an unconscious suspect, and now they find out there is another way into the ICU, and obviously someone masquerading as a detective is trying to gain access to their man. It was a situation where Ryan didn't want to leave, if Hendrickson woke up, he wanted to be there, and if this woman came back, he wanted to be there as well. He sat down into a chair along the wall, and put his head in his hands.

"Shit, I'm tired," he said to himself.

Don walked back up to him, "someone is on the way up from downstairs, you ok?"

"No I'm not ok, I feel like I've been beat with a stick, and there doesn't seem to be any way we can get what we need. This case has me dragging, Don. We need a break, and we need it quick. The whole city is on edge, and we're the one's that have to bring it back to normal."

"You're putting too much pressure on yourself, we'll get this guy or woman, whoever is doing it."

Ryan looked up at Don, he looked as tired as Ryan felt, but he was still the optimist; still the one that was saying, lets go. Ryan stood up, and the two men walked down the hall to the nurse's station.

He left explicit instructions with the nurse to call them if and when this woman returned, then went to the operating room, and gave instructions to the officer that had come up from the lobby. Ryan handed him a clipboard with paper on it.

"Anyone coming in here will sign this, and you *will* see their identification, match it with their driver's license. I've talked with the hospital administration, and they assure me that no one will be coming in here except authorized personnel. If you see anything you think is unusual, call me and let me know."

It seemed the only thing left to do was wait, neither of them was sure what they were waiting for, but they would wait nonetheless. Both decided that waiting at the hospital was an attempt at futility, and they should call it a day, and head for home. Being away from Hendrickson wasn't going to be easy, but neither would be any good to the situation as tired as they were.

Chapter Twenty

Scooter sat in his small living room polishing his nickel-plated .357 he had gotten when he was a teenager. He loved the pistol, and treated it with fascination and care, much like many gun owners did to prized pieces worth hundreds more than this pistol. He had done it so many times he didn't even look at the gun anymore while he worked. He just stared at the small TV in the corner, rubbing the gun gently between his hands. He inadvertently pulled the hammer back, and clicked it shut, as he cleaned the barrel. Every once in a while he would put the gun up in the air as if he were getting ready to shoot it at something. He spun the cylinder sometimes, not even knowing he was doing it; the whole procedure was second nature to him. His smile was ear to ear the entire time.

On the table of the living room sat three die cast scale model cars. One was Dale Earnhardt Jr, one was an old Michael Waltrip *NAPA* car, and the other was his favorite, the Intimidator, Dale Earnhardt. The latter was autographed on the top, and was poised proudly underneath a custom-built glass case. The black body glistening in the light of the lamp across the room, it was a thing of beauty in his eyes, and one of the few things he owned that had any value at all.

Like the gun, he revered the pleasure of looking at, and touching the car. He didn't care if the new NASCAR fans didn't remember Earnhardt, he did, and he still remembered watching him as he grew up, and remembered the day he died at Daytona with vivid recollection. Scooter had gone into a deep depression when Earnhardt was killed, many other fans of the racing icon reacted the same way, almost to the point of seclusion from the world. He lost his job, and couldn't pay his rent for that month, which took some quick talking to get out of, but as always he took the road of conning his landlady until she retreated back to her house at the front of the park. He would sneak in the back way until he had stolen enough money to pay her what was due. It was a miserable month. Finally he got out of his slump, and got a job at a local garage, changing oil for customers.

The trailer he lived in was small; perhaps tiny was a better word for it. It was perched in a grove of trees at the backside of the trailer park, and was surrounded by junk cars, and empty beer cans. If you walked through the park at night, which wasn't a great idea, you would here the screaming of several women in different stages of distress, as they tried to get their husbands to stop watching television or one of the kids to do something.

He had two bedrooms, but neither was livable. They were filled with old newspaper boxes from several different papers in the area, the kind of boxes you put your 50-cents into, and get the daily reading. Scooter was proud of how he figured out how to get the quarters out of them, that is once he got them in the back of his truck, and brought them home. The only thing he hadn't figured out was what to do with them once he got the money out, so he just stacked them in the rooms. Now he had so many of them that he couldn't use either bedroom, he even had one in the bathroom. Some of the newspapers went back as far as six-months, but he still read them while he did his business every morning.

He put the gun back in the small corner table he had his lamp on, lifted the glass top off of the case and picked up the Dale Earnhardt car. He dug out a special dusting rag, and started to shine the car much like he did the gun. There weren't many things he was proud of, but this car was his prize, he honestly loved it. He stared intently at the television while he gently rubbed the scaled piece of NASCAR history. He looked down at the car at the same time he heard the news come on. He picked up the remote, and tried to change the channel, but the battery was low, and the remote did nothing. He hit it on his knee. Sometimes that brought it back to life and it would work; he pointed it at the same time a picture of Roger Fallon was flashed on the screen. He immediately put the remote down, and listened to the news lady explain what happened to what she called, "one of East Tennessee's leading citizens."

"Mr. Fallon was allegedly pointing a gun in the food court of the mall at this young girl," a picture of Aubrey was prominently displayed on the TV screen, "when the police spotted him, killing him before he could get to his alleged victim," she said in her matter of fact voice. "The motive for the attempted murder is still under investigation," she continued.

Scooter dropped his prize car on the floor, causing one of the wheels to go flying in the opposite direction. He stood up, and headed to the back of the trailer to his dresser. He started to sweat immediately while he grabbed what few necessities he had. He had to get out of there, go somewhere, he wasn't sure where, but he had to leave. Massey said he would take care of the girl, and he was dead, now Fallon tried, and he was dead too. Scooter didn't care about the girl anymore; if he hung around he knew he would be next. He rummaged through the piles of dirty clothes, looking for anything that was somewhat clean. He looked around the room as he tossed clothes around in his search, throwing them into a trash bag that was lying in the room. His mind racing about how to get to wherever he was going.

Once he had a sufficient stash of his cleanest, dirty clothes, he headed back to the front of the trailer, reached into the table, and grabbed his gun, stuffing it into his pants. He looked around the room, and saw the Earnhardt car scattered on the floor. His prize possession was now junk, he picked up the wheel that had flown across the room, and fondled it with forlorn passion. He stuck it in his pocket, and opened the door with his back to it. When he turned, directly in front of him, standing in the doorway was a well-dressed woman, staring at him with his trash bag thrown over his shoulder.

"Planning a trip, Scooter?" she said.

His surprise showed on his face, but she took no time to notice, she jabbed the needle deep into his arm. He instantly felt the effects of the drug as his body started to go limp. His vision blurred, and he slipped down to his knees, dropping the trash bag as he went. He felt her hand go under his arm as she tried to pick him up from the floor. He half walked, and was half carried outside, the cold air taking his senses by surprise. He felt himself being put into a car, the dome light stabbing at his blurring eyes, then it was black, he felt nothing, and saw nothing more.

She smiled as they drove out of the park, and down the road toward Knoxville. Her ace in the hole was being played, and she had no intention of giving up the hand. Scooter snored restfully on the other side of the car, not knowing what had just hit him. Stupid little Scooter was so ready to run when he heard of Fallon's death. So ready to step into what she now needed him for. Her original intention was just to kill him, and go on her way, but Ben changed the rules with his escape, and she had to come up with another plan to aid in her quest. Some might have called it greed, but she had to finish what she started, and Ben was one of the biggest pieces of the puzzle. Scooter would unwittingly play a part in his demise as well.

The drive was uneventful as they worked their way through the streets of Knoxville, eventually pulling up in front of the building she now called home. It was a close call when Ben escaped, but he got just far enough out of the area of the loft to insure the police wouldn't find where he had come from. If she played her cards right, she could stop him from talking, and keep the promise she had made to herself, and use Scooter to do it. Timing was the entire issue, simple timing, not a simple plan, but simple timing. She reached over, and slapped Scooter hard on the face. He jerked his head up, but didn't wake.

"Wake up!" she yelled, and again he stirred.

She didn't want him awake to complete consciousness, but she needed him awake enough that she could aid him in walking up to the room where she had held Ben earlier. He was small, but still too big for her to carry. She got out of the car, went to the other side, and opened the door. Scooter didn't fall, he just kind of indolently moved his head upward, one eye was open, and the other closed. She took him under his arm, and the two climbed from the car, into the building.

After she laid him on the floor in the room, and placed duct tape on his mouth, she went into her bedroom, and flopped on the bed. Her head was spinning wildly with exhaustion. She couldn't move, even enough to take her clothes off, and climb under the blanket. She did manage to flip the bedspread over on top of her, and as quickly as it was done, started to doze into that spot between sleep, and reality.

Her mind was as restless as her body was listless. She could hear traffic on the street, but she couldn't have heard someone talking in the same room. Her mind began to dream that she was standing on the street outside the loft on a hazy warm day. She thought it was strange the heat and humidity had returned so quickly after the cold that had gripped the city for the past few weeks. The haze was thick, and it was hard to see the end of the street she was standing on. Out of the haze a young girl slowly walked toward her. She could see her outline, but couldn't make out her face or features. She was like a walking shadow in the mist. The figure kept walking until it was almost even with where she was standing in front of the loft. When the figure got there, she felt the fear surround her, and she reached out to comfort the blackness of the shadow. The young girl moved backward at her touch, and turned her head. For the first time she saw the figures face, it was Aubrey; her beautiful eyes staring blankly back at her. She reached out her hand once again, and as before the figure retreated away, this time further back so she could barely see her features again. She tried to speak, but nothing would come out, she was mute, and the figure wouldn't let her help. Suddenly the figure started walking away, her back to her as it walked the opposite direction, but still her face was visible, her eyes bright as ever. A calm came over her as the figure got further and further down the street, but just as she was starting to feel the serenity of peace, a giant hand swooped down, and swept Aubrey away, into the darkness with an evil laugh.

She sprung up in her bed, wide-awake again, sweat pouring from everywhere on her body. She wiped her forehead, and looked around the room, half to verify where she was, and half to see if what happened in the dream could have been real. She looked at the clock on the headboard; it had been an hour since she had lay down, and slipped into the nightmare of dreamland.

She got up, and went into the kitchen for a drink of water. She took a quick moment to look in the door to the room where Scooter was passed out on the floor. She wouldn't make the same mistake twice, this time she would watch her captive prey, and insure the door remained locked. It was a stupid oversight with Ben, and frankly she didn't think he had it in him to escape. This time she would not underestimate her prisoner.

He was still unconscious, and hadn't moved since she had placed him in the room. Her exhaustion was starting to catch back up with her as she drank the cold water. She leaned on the counter, and thought of what she had to do next. The day ahead would be one of the most important of the mission she had chosen for herself. She finished the water, took another look at the clock, and headed back to the bedroom. This time she would shower, get into proper bedclothes, and slip into the sheets for restful sleep. Her guilt had been presented tonight, now she had to put it aside, and revitalize her body and spirit.

Chapter Twenty-One

Ryan was awake long after he and his wife had made love, love that was hard for Ryan considering the day's events. His life away from work had to continue, and he had promised himself and Laura, he would leave work, at work. Sometimes it was tough, almost impossible, but for the most part, he did it with unwanted guilt.

He had arrived at his house the second time that night far later than the first. It was well after midnight, but the lights in the house shined brightly, and he was surprised with a dinner by candlelight and roses. Laura had gone to great lengths to help him forget the day, after he had called her, and she could hear the stress in his voice. The dinner was wonderful, and Ryan felt some of his anxiety start to slip away as he went upstairs and kissed his young son in his crib. He had paused for some time with him, watching him breath deeply in the sleepy land of whatever it is that baby's dream. Josh would twitch every once in a while, and his eyes were searching for the unreachable dream under his eyelids, moving back and forth, and up and down. It was peaceful, and touching as he sat next to his crib and stroked his back. He brushed back Josh's hair, and leaned into the crib to kiss his son gently on the cheek, his pride of him almost overwhelming.

When he had finished the bonding session with his son, he came downstairs to another surprise. Laura was sitting on the couch with a glass of wine in her hand and nothing on her body, romantically inviting

Ryan to some much-needed comfort in her arms. The two made love on the couch, and then went up to their room for the second session, never once leaving each other's arms, as they walked up the stairs.

Now he was wide-awake, with his arms behind his head, laying on his back listening to his wife sleep in total satisfaction of having made the early morning a memory that would remain forever in his mind. He would have never guessed that his day would end with such beauty and joy. He slowly tried to let his mind go, and welcome the rest he so badly needed. Several things went through his mind, but eventually his eyelids became heavy, and his mind forgot most of the thoughts he worked so hard on during the pervious day.

Sleep came within minutes after he remembered thinking that it would be hard to fall into his dreamland. It was late, but his rest was deep, and his mind made no effort to dream, and his body didn't move.

It seemed as though eight o'clock came fast after his last thought, but the alarm was forceful, and he relented with a whack on the top of it. Almost simultaneously his phone started ringing, and he was forced to beam up to the world of the living.

Laura reached over him, and grabbed the phone, dropping it on his chest, and then fumbling it to her ear, "he's not here," she said with a sleepy voice.

"Let me have it honey," he said and took it from her.

Don was laughing on the other end, "damn buddy, get her to do your dirty work every morning, maybe you'll get that vacation after all."

Ryan sat up on the headboard, repositioned the phone, and gave Don a half-hearted hello, "what's up buddy?" he asked.

"I'm already over at the hospital, and you may want to get over here soon. Hendrickson woke up last night, and they say he was all talk. They gave him a weak sedative, and say that he will be out of it soon. I think we might want to be the first one's to see what he has to say. Besides, if that woman police officer returns, you might want to talk with her," he gave Ryan a half-hearted laugh knowing he was saying something that Ryan may take as an insult.

"I'll be there in a little while you smart ass," Ryan told him. "You just make damn sure no one else gets in that room, you got that?"

Ryan got up from the bed, and did his morning routine while Laura tried to grab the extra few minutes of sleep that comes before a busy day. There wasn't a sound coming from Josh's room, so she was safe for the time being. He gave her a kiss on the forehead, and headed out the door for the drive to UT Medical Center and an interview that he didn't look forward to.

The morning news on the radio was full of the mundane and horrible things that happen in the world while others slept. He listened intently when his case was mentioned, but there were no new developments, and Ryan was proud that his friend had kept his word, not leaking anything he had said to others. When he finally drove up into the parking area for the hospital, he noticed that there were a number of police cars still parked at the entrance to the lobby. There were numerous uniformed policemen mulling around, with hospital staff, and patients outside the doors, lots of them, looking around as if they didn't know what was happening. People in hospital gowns were sitting on the curb with nurses and doctors alike, hovering over them. He hurriedly parked the car right where he was driving, and left it with the door open, running to the front door.

"What the hell happened here?" he said to no one in particular.

He looked around frantically, as two other detectives walked up to him, "apparently there are several bombs inside Rose," one of the men told him. "They have a minimal staff inside to watch the ICU patients, and some in the emergency room, but everyone else is out. We were just trying to call you when you drove up."

"When did the call come in?" he asked, as he looked around for Don.

"About fifteen minutes ago. We've contacted the other hospitals in the area in case we have to evacuate the critical patients, but Breeding called down from the ICU, and told us to wait until he gave us the ok. Sammons is on the way."

Ryan moved quickly toward the front door of the hospital, and went inside. A uniformed officer stepped in front of him, but only for a quick second, then thought better of the move, and shuffled aside when he saw the resolve in the detectives face. Ryan thought he knew what was going on, and he was going to get to Don before it escalated to something bigger that no one would be able to handle. He headed up the stairs to the ICU, drawing his gun, as he took the steps two at a time. When he reached the floor that the ICU was located on he paused, and readied for the entrance into what might be danger.

He opened the door slowly, just peeking through a small gap that he made. Down the hall he could see nothing, only empty hallway. He shoved the door to its fully open position, and carefully looked down the opposite way in the hallway. There he saw two bodies laying motionless in the middle, one face down, and one in a crumpled lump. He could tell that one of the bodies must have been a nurse, her colored smock half covering her head, blood circling her in a crimson ring. The other body was the officer that Don and he had been talking with the night before. His gun drawn, but still in his hand, it appeared as if he never had the chance to fire it.

Slowly, and cautiously he slipped down the hall, with his back against the handrail that ran on the wall. The ICU doors were closed, so he crouched until he reached the nurse. He felt her neck for a pulse, and found nothing. He moved slowly to the officer, and got the same result. He pulled out his cell phone, and dialed the number to the Chief of Detectives.

The chief immediately answered, "Rose, what the hell are you doing, you know—," Ryan quickly but quietly interrupted the chief, "there are two dead already Chief," he said almost in a whisper, "I'm outside the ICU, there is no bomb, it was diversion to get to Hendrickson, send me backup. Do it quietly, but quickly."

There was no response, but Ryan knew the chief understood what he was talking about and what he needed. He flipped his phone closed, and stood back up against the wall taking a deep breath. His first inclination was to go through the door and see what was on the other side. His concern was, of course, for his partner. If Hendrickson was dead, that was something they could deal with, but losing Don was something unacceptable to him. If someone were willing to kill the policeman that was at his feet, they wouldn't hesitate to take the rest of the room with him.

He knew waiting was the thing his superiors would expect, and certainly want him to do; there was protocol after all. Waiting was something most law enforcement would find extremely hard to do, as it was for him.

He heard something move inside the room, and his decision was made for him. If he waited, Don may be killed while he stood in the hallway, it was a chance he had to take, and take swiftly. He took one more deep breath, and pressed the button on the wall that opened the door to the ICU. He sprung around the corner, and quickly put himself against the wall again. In the room there were several beds that were empty, and some had patients in them. One man just inside the door looked as if he had seen a ghost, tubes coming out of almost every orifice in his body, and even with that his eyes were wide open. He was glaring at Ryan as he slipped into the unit. Everything was deathly quiet; only the sound of heart monitors broke the eerie, lonesome silence. Ryan worked his way to the back of the room where he remembered Hendrickson being located the night before. The curtain was closed around his bed, as was the one next to it. Ryan tried to remember if there was anyone next to Ben when they had seen him last, but he couldn't, he just didn't pay that close of attention when he and Don were there.

He slipped back the curtain to look at the patient inside. An elderly lady was in the bed, but everything had been pulled from her. Wires, and tubes hung precariously around the bed, and her stare indicated she no longer needed any of them anyway. Ryan moved next to her bed, and put his foot out to kick the curtains back so he could view what was behind them, again he took a deep breath and performed the task. He had his gun up even with his face, but immediately noticed he didn't need it, everything in the space was gone, the bed, the monitors, the IV unit, everything, including Hendrickson. He went to the next space, and threw open the curtain; there was a bed, but no patient inside of it, it was freshly made, and not housing anyone. He put his gun down, but kept it in his hands as he started to walk around the rest of the room, looking, searching for Don, or Hendrickson. It was then he noticed there were no medical personnel in the room, not one. Either they had fled or were taken. He turned just as a uniformed officer came in the door on the other side of the room, gun at the ready and pointing in Ryan's direction. He immediately recognized him, and withdrew his weapon, as an army of officer's, followed with the staff of the hospital, came in behind him. Chief Detective Bob Sammons was close behind them.

"You ever pull a stunt like this again Rose, and I swear I'll have your badge," he scolded. "What did you find in here?"

"Nothing, that's the problem, nothing, Hendrickson is gone, and so is Don, all the medical staff is missing also."

Sammons indicated with the wave of his hand for officers to spread out, and start looking for the missing men and staff that were supposed to be in the unit. They left in sweeping turns out into the hallways, as Sammons radioed down to the others, still located on the streets, and in ambulances to stay put for the time being. He couldn't risk anyone walking into a situation they couldn't handle, "come with me Ryan, where do you think they would go from here?"

Sammons stayed on his radio, giving instructions for all the exits to be closed down, making sure no one left the interior of the hospital, or came back in, and then the two headed for the ground floor.

When they reached the elevators an officer stepped out with a business card in his hands, "I found this on the floor of the elevator, and thought I should bring it to you right away."

Ryan took the card, printed in the standard detective print was "Don Breeding" across the center. Ryan knew immediately the card was placed with a purpose, the purpose of showing Ryan where he was going. He instantly went to work looking on the floor for the next sign of where Don was taking them, or where she was taking him.

Chapter Twenty-Two

It hadn't been easy slipping into the ICU without someone noticing, as a matter of fact, it had come at a great expense in her eyes. An innocent person had to die, of course it wasn't the first, the electrician was also an innocent victim, but at least he played a part in the eventual death of Harold Massey. That much she could take solace in, unfortunately, the elderly woman lying in her bed awaiting death played no part, except that her alarms had gotten too loud, and she couldn't risk the attention.

That was all in the past now, as for the present, she walked behind Detective Breeding while he wheeled her unconscious ex-husband down the corridor on the rolling hospital bed he had been sleeping on. Passed out was probably a better way to describe his condition, he was drugged, and by the look on his face it was a state in which he enjoyed being.

They were almost caught up with the rest of the patients being evacuated from the hospital after the bomb threat was called in. She had devised the plan after waking up, and checking on Scooter, tied up in the same room Ben had escaped from. He made several sounds as he tried to get himself out of his bindings, but she was confident he would remain in his shackles until it was time for her to release him. She double-checked the lock, and then drove to the pay phone on the street in front of UT Medical Center.

She made the call to the hospital administrator, and made it very clear there were several bombs placed strategically throughout the corridors on several of the floors. Her knowledge of the hospital had convinced him that it was not a crank call, that the threat could be serious. Therefore he had ordered the evacuation. Her presumption was it would take hours to check it all out, and time would give her the chance she needed to get to Ben.

When she arrived on the ICU floor a nurse that stayed behind was first to object to her being in the corridor leading to the door. She had told her she needed to leave immediately or she would make sure the police would remove her. When she put the knife in her, the policeman came lunging at her, gun in hand, but her needle was faster than his trigger finger, and again she was able to render an adversary helpless. Unfortunately the needle had more in it than she intended to give him and he died quickly of an overdose, and unintentional overdose, but dead just the same. A man that was the first patient in the unit watched the entire episode, trying to assist, but was unable to move out of the bed his sickness had shackled him to. He just lay there with his eyes wide open, blinking as if it would make everything go away. She thought he looked pitiful in his helplessness.

When she found Ben, the good detective had been sitting with his back to the space the old lady was in, so she worked her way by the curtain, and quickly got behind Breeding. She took out a new needle, and placed it against the back of his neck. He never tried to go for his pistol, and she was able to persuade him that he should hand it over to her. She also convinced him to call his superiors, and let them know that he had a handle on the situation in the unit. That was when the old lady started her convulsions, perhaps she had set her off into the series of events; she wasn't sure. The alarms started going off, and the old lady went completely rigid at first, so she pulled the plug on the monitor. The silence was only for an instant as the alarm on the respirator went off, and finally she just started pulling all the plugs, she didn't have time to check each one. Without any struggle at all, the elderly lady passed quickly, she probably never knew what hit her. Of course none of that was planned, but it's amazing how much you can improvise when you are desperate.

Her desperation was coming at a high expense, she knew that she would probably not survive after all that she had done, but everything had been worth it so far. She was able to rid the world of several of the worst men she knew of, and it didn't cost the tax paying public a dime so far. No trials, and no public defenders, no humiliation for her daughter, and they wouldn't have to eat off the public for the rest of their lives. She was almost proud of herself, especially after she had promised to come back and get Aubrey, but had reneged on that promise.

After she had left Ben, and promptly divorced him, she returned to, and finished nursing school. It was a goal she had set for herself before she met him. After she graduated, she landed a job in a reputable doctor's office close to UT. Her guilt over not returning to Aubrey seemed to become less every day, thinking Aubrey was doing fine without her. Going back to get her was something she really had intentions of doing, and she was going to as soon as she got settled in a new place. Time seemed to slip away, and she justified to herself that Aubrey was fine with her father; she didn't need to be uprooted. That was until she had lunch with her friend Melissa from Dr. Cranston's office one day.

"Loraine," she had said, "I heard the doctor talking with two of his friends in his office this morning, I wasn't supposed to listen, but I couldn't help it. He told them to meet him at some guy named Hendrickson's house tonight, so they could do things with the man's daughter, specific things," she looked down at the table with an embarrassed look on her face.

"I was appalled, but I couldn't say anything to him. I'm sick over it, I think I'll quit next week if I can't figure out what to do," again she looked down, and a tear splashed onto the table.

Melissa didn't know that Loraine was, or used to be Hendrickson's wife. She had taken her maiden name, Bullock, when she went back to school, and really didn't care if she ever heard Ben Hendrickson's name again, but Aubrey, that was a different story. The guilt immediately returned. Loraine thought about going to the police, but decided that it would just end up in court, the men would be tried and do their time, but Aubrey would suffer the humiliation for the rest of her life. She decided that this way, her way, no one would have to pay for these degenerates to eat or house them in a prison; they would be under the earth, where they belonged.

Loraine wasn't sure how to console her friend, but she was absolutely sure how to rectify the situation with Dr. Cranston. She had visited Cranston's wife, and told her of what she thought was going on with Ben. Evelyn Cranston hadn't seen Loraine in a long time, and seemed to shrug most of it off, but after a few questions about where he was late at night, and whether he was acting strange in any way, she looked like she just may have believed her. Plans were made that day in the Congresswoman's office, now Loraine was sticking to her part of the plan.

She did her research, and found out the names of all the scum that had been coming and going at the house, and vowed that she would make it even. She would take care of them her way, for her daughter. She also vowed that Ben would pay, and his payment would be living in prison for the rest of his life with the knowledge that she did all of this, that she came back for Aubrey.

Now it had come down to this, she had just kidnapped a Knoxville detective, and forced him to help her get Ben out of the hospital. The whole thing was supposed to be cleaner than it was now, her plan was steady, firm and without glitches, unfortunately, this detective and his partner, had muddied up the water. It wasn't that she hadn't planned on the police getting involved; of course she knew that would happen. What she hadn't planned on was them getting in touch with Aubrey so quickly, and then taking Ben to the hotel, where she had to get him so she could continue with her plan.

The three had come down the corridor with the medical staff that was left behind to take care of the critical patients. She made Don lock them in one of the doctor's offices, and then started to make their way to the parking garage, where she had her car waiting.

Don wasn't a willing participant in this series of events, but decided that he should go along with her for a while; maybe he would be able to learn something about the whole mess. He hadn't figured on her coming as early to the hospital as she did. She had come up from behind, and forced him to take Ben with them, forced him to call his superiors, and then forced him to help her take Hendrickson out of the hospital. She had put the needle to his neck, thinking that she shouldn't sink it too far in, she had, and a small amount of whatever she had in it had made him dizzy enough to affect his balance. It was enough to make him a little woozy, and a bit off balance, but not enough to affect his judgment.

After she had slipped up from behind, his role changed, from one of guard to one as a victim he supposed. His thoughts were now centered on where and when he could overpower her, and wrap this entire affair up. His hands were full with the bed, and the towers that held the IV that was connected to Hendrickson's arm. The nurse had told him when he got there that morning that the sedation would wear off soon, but now he hoped that it would be longer than what they thought. He didn't need a panicking maniac; along with what he thought was a crazy lady, in this situation. When they walked along the corridor, he tried to leave small signs for Ryan to follow them, pieces that would be evident to his partner as to where they were headed. He had dropped one of his business cards in the elevator, thinking that if she noticed it he would simply pick it up and go on. She didn't, and his hope now was that they got the same elevator, or they would search them, and someone would find it. He had dropped two more as they hurried down some corridors. Her attention was more on how fast they could move rather than his dropping things along the way.

They reached the parking garage, and stepped into the cold, it was crisp enough that it almost took his breath away. She had taken them without jackets, so he wore only his shirt with a tie. The three crept down until she found her car, which was parked close to the elevators; it was an SUV that would easily fit Ben into it.

Don parked the bed behind the SUV, and stood for a moment. She pressed the button on the key ring, and the vehicle came to life with its lights flashing, and a brief honk of the horn. The back tailgate came up slowly to reveal where Ben would spend his next few minutes or hours he suspected.

"Get him off of the bed, and put him in there," she demanded.

Don slowly picked Hendrickson up off of the bed, and started to lay him in the back of the car. He stirred slightly, and opened his eyes for a brief moment, but immediately went back to the state he was in. Don laid him down, and took the IV bottle off the stand, and laid it next to him. Hendrickson didn't move.

"Now what?" Don asked. "Do you think you can just drive out of here with him?"

"Who's going to stop me, look around, everyone is concerned about the hospital, and there isn't anyone here that even cares about these cars."

She was right; all the action was in the front of the hospital, and around the doors leading in and out of it. No one was in the parking garage, and Don suspected that they had cleared it, and simply left it alone while they searched inside. He searched with his peripheral vision, trying not to take his eyes off of his captor at the same time.

She closed the door on the car, moving backwards a couple of inches to avoid being hit in the head with it. When she did, Don thought he could make his move, and he quickly started toward her. His swing was swift, and if it would have connected it would have certainly rendered her unconscious, but his arm got nothing but air as she saw it coming, and moved at the last instant. He lost his balance, only momentarily, but swerved none-the-less, running into the bed that Hendrickson had been on. The bed went rolling, and she swung around behind him jabbing the needle hard into his arm. He pulled away before she could get the full amount of the drug dispensed, but it was enough that he immediately couldn't see where he was looking, then everything started to spin. He fell to his knees, and grabbed at the needle still sticking out of his arm. A small spot of blood formed in the material of his shirt as he took the needle out. He looked at it as if it were some sort of item he couldn't understand. He went the rest of the way to the ground, sitting back on his heels, swinging back and forth in a drunken manner. He could see her opening the door to the car, and getting in. It was funny to him that it really did look like it was in slow motion, like he had heard of all these years. He was helpless, awake, but unable to move under his own power. He hadn't fallen all the way yet, but sat there, his butt on his heels, swinging in a slow circle with the needle in his hands. He was thinking hard about a way that he could stop the car as it drove away in a blur. His mind working, but his body stopped in a stupor on the ground.

Finally he couldn't stay in the position any longer, and fell to his side. He could feel the cold concrete on his skin as he tried to straighten his legs. He closed his eyes, and thought to himself that he didn't want to lose consciousness. He needed to stay awake, and make some sort of sound so someone could find him. He fumbled around, and dropped the needle next to him, trying to get in his pocket for his cell phone. It was no use, he was losing control of his arms and legs, and things were going more and more into a blur.

Ryan reached the parking garage just as Don slipped down into a prone position. The officer that had found the business card in the elevator was close behind them, he now held three of the cards that Don had dropped in his, *Hansel and Gretel,* style message. It didn't take him long to figure out where she was taking his partner, but it was a surprise to find him on the floor of the garage, needle next to him, barely awake.

He got his cell phone out, "get someone up here to the third floor of the parking garage, now!" he yelled into the phone, and at the same time the officer was calling on his radio.

Ryan tried to help Don into a sitting position, and moved him over to the wall, leaning him against it, "hang in there, buddy, someone's on the way," Ryan told him.

Don tried to lift his arm and indicate the direction that the car had driven away, but merely got a sloppy movement out of it. He resigned himself to just remaining there; watching everything go on in slow motion. He could hear Ryan talking to him, but didn't understand a thing he said. He thought that it was one of the strangest feelings he could remember ever having.

An ambulance arrived a short time later, and they loaded him in, and whisked him off to the emergency entrance of the hospital. The EMT indicated that it was his excellent physical shape that allowed him to even be awake. His day was complete with his admittance into the place he was just trying to save. What a start to the day.

Ryan stood next to Sammons in the parking garage as the ambulance went toward the exit, "we need to find this broad," he said. "We need to find her quick, lets go look at the tapes of the cars leaving the garage, and find out where she's going," both walking toward the parking garage office.

The two stood back in the office of the parking garage, and watched the videotape on the monitor. A dark colored SUV left the building, then turned left onto Neyland Drive. She drove toward the downtown area.

"Stop the tape, and see if you can get the plate number," he told the attendant.

The three squinted, and Ryan was barely able to read the number on the Tennessee plate gracing the back of the car. He wrote it down, and handed it to an officer that was standing just outside the door. He immediately got on his radio, and called the plate number into the office for identification.

"I'm going down to the emergency room, and see if they've made any progress with Don," Ryan told Sammons. "If anyone calls, let me know, I'm waiting for the results on the search around where they found Hendrickson, he had to be kept somewhere around there, he wasn't in any shape to walk far."

He hadn't gotten ten steps away from the small office when Sammons called him back, they've found something that you might be very interested in Ryan, he handed him a piece of paper that had just been handed to the Chief.

Next to the plate number was written a name "Evelyn Cranston", underneath the plate number and name, was an address. The address was located two blocks from where Ben Hendrickson was found on the street. Next to the address was the name again, "Evelyn Cranston".

Ryan looked at Sammons in a kind of puzzling but surprised way. He shoved the paper into his pocket, and turned to walk to the emergency room where Don was being treated. After he saw that his partner, his friend, was doing fine, he was making a trip to see Evelyn Cranston at her home. The address was too close to be a coincidence; he felt a trip there would allow some needed answers.

"Damn," he said out loud to himself, "Damn!" He broke into a fast walk.

Loraine struggled trying to get Ben out of the elevator with his body almost completely limp. The only thing that allowed her to move him was the little help he gave with the occasional shuffle of his legs. She kept prodding him to try to walk, but the effect of the sedative must have been stronger than what the nurses expected. He giggled a couple of times in the car, and even laughed openly when she had taken him out of the back seat. An older man that looked as though he was homeless had helped her when he saw Ben wasn't cooperating with the journey out of the car. Her lie was convincing about having too much to drink at an office lunch get together, so he agreed to assist her. She had allowed the man to help as far as the elevator, and then gave him a couple of dollars, and he was on his way, probably to the liquor store, by the smell of his breath.

She didn't want to risk the two men together in the same small room for fear they could work together, so she placed Ben on the floor, got some plastic tie straps from the drawer, and put them around his wrists and ankles. She had seen the police use the straps to subdue criminals on television, so she thought they would do just fine for her drugged up ex husband.

He would be fine until it was time for her to finish both of the men off, she thought to herself. It wouldn't be long now until all of the scum she had set out to rid the world of would be gone, and Aubrey would be safe again.

Chapter Twenty-Three

Aubrey and Amy stood in front of the television set watching the news as it detailed how the threat of a bomb at UT Medical Center had turned into the kidnapping of a suspect in the string of murders in Knoxville. The reporter indicated that the suspect was Ben Hendrickson, a man that had been reported missing for the past few days, and how another citizen had found him on the street in the downtown area and alerted authorities.

"Wow," Amy commented with surprised on her face, "that's your Dad, Aubrey, they found him."

Aubrey turned away from the television, and grabbed her coat, "I've got to find Detective Rose," she said, as she headed for the front door.

Amy called out to her mom in the next room, and Sara came immediately to the door to stop Aubrey from leaving the house. She reached out, and stopped the door from opening with her arm then stepped in front of Aubrey.

"I need to find Detective Rose," Aubrey told her, as she tried to hold back the tears.

"Honey, I know you think you need to see your father, and I know that you are going through things that I will never understand, but please let me help you with this. Let me call Detective Rose, and see what his feelings are. If he thinks you should come, I'm sure he will let us know."

Sara looked into Aubrey's eyes, and saw the hurt and fear compile together. Finally, Aubrey let go as she fell into Sara's arms, and sobbed. She wasn't sure if the sobs were for Ben or for her. Amy started to cry also, more for Aubrey's pain than that of her father's predicament; Sara knew that. She walked her back into the living room, and sat Aubrey on the sofa with Amy close behind. Then she went to the phone, and dialed Ryan Rose's cell phone.

Ryan was driving far too fast for the road conditions in Knoxville, but his sense of urgency had been ignited with the disappearance of Ben Hendrickson, and the drugging of his partner back at the hospital. He was on his way to the home of Evelyn Cranston; to find out what part she played in each of the incidents. He knew it was no coincidence that her vehicle was used in the abduction. She was involved, and it was time to find out what that involvement was.

He stopped at traffic light at the same time his cell-phone rang, "Detective Rose," he said immediately.

"Ryan," Don was on the other end. "They've released me from the hospital, well not really released me, let's just say that I convinced them to let me go. I got to Sammons before he left, and we're both coming to meet you. We've called Congresswoman Cranston's office, and she's in Washington until next week. We took a closer look at the picture from the parking garage, and that isn't Cranston in the car, it is a woman, but we can't identify her from that photo. Wait for us before you go inside that house. If there is anyone in there, we'll need some backup."

Ryan's phone beeped, and indicated he had another call coming in. He ignored it, and continued with Don, "listen buddy, you don't have to come over here, if they want you to stay there, you do that."

"I'm fine now, just a little light headed is all, and we're on our way, just a few minutes behind you."

Ryan hung up his phone, and looked to see if the other call was still on the line, but they had already hung up with no message.

Sara put the phone back down, and stared blankly through the two girls standing in front of her. Rose hadn't answered, and it didn't seem like a good idea to leave him a message.

Aubrey broke her blank expression, "did he answer," she asked with urgency.

"No," Sara responded quietly. "We'll call him in a few minutes, and see what he wants us to do."

"I have to go Sara," Aubrey pleaded to her. "I can't help it, I need to know if he's alive or dead!"

Sara again looked as though she were looking through the girls instead of at them. She stood up, "both of you get your coats, we'll find Detective Rose, and we'll start at the police station where he took us before.

Sara wasn't sure what she and the two girls were looking for or if they would find it with Detective Rose. What she did know was that Aubrey was very upset over the television report, and it was up to her to make sure she was able to remain as calm as possible. She had a hard time understanding Aubrey's concern for Ben. After all, he was the one that had caused her all this pain and suffering. She supposed that even with all that had happened, Aubrey couldn't let go of the only parent she thought she had left. When they got in the car, she tried his cell-phone again, this time it rang only once, and Ryan answered.

"Detective, this is Sara Temple. Aubrey and Amy saw a report that Ben was found, but was kidnapped again, is it true?"

"Mrs. Temple, yea it's true. We're not sure who it is at this point, but it was a woman. I assure you if we find out anything else we'll call you."

"Aubrey is upset, she wants to come to see you, and help if she can," Sara told him.

Ryan listened on the other end, and thought for a couple of moments before he replied, "I don't think it's a good idea to come here, can she wait for me at the station?"

"I think she needs to be there, as a matter of fact I think she needs to be there badly, detective," Sara was almost pleading with him.

Ryan was almost at the house as they spoke, and finally gave in, telling Sara the address of the house, agreeing that Aubrey may need to come in case they needed her to help with negotiations. He thought she might be of help with the kidnapper, especially if there was some sort of connection between the two ladies. He was apprehensive about letting them come to what he believed would be a scene, but with Don on the way, he thought he could keep the ladies in a safe position.

He pulled up across the street from the loft as the sun was setting in the west. He started to get out of the car, and go to the door without waiting for his boss and his partner, but thought better of it. Sammons was clear after he had gone into the hospital without permission that this wasn't to happen again. He withdrew his hand from the door handle, and slid down a little in the seat of the car. He thought to himself that the wait wouldn't be long, and that it would probably be worth the patience.

Inside the loft, Loraine was preparing for the final phase of her mission. She had two men to finish, and if it was going to happen, she felt as if she needed to add some urgency to her plight.

First she went to the small door on the other side of the kitchen, and confirmed that it was indeed still locked. Her paranoia for this was from Ben's earlier escape from the same room that Scooter was in at the moment. Scooter hadn't made a sound since she had been there, so she was inclined to open the door, but decided against it for fear he may have escaped his bindings, and lay in wait for her to do just that. With the lock on the door, the room was more than secure. In addition to the two locks on the door, she had also bolted the bottom with a long lock that went into the floor of the loft. It was something that had always been there, but using it was always a pain, so she usually left it in the upright position. If he did escape, he would have a hard time knocking the wooden door down. She decided to leave well enough alone, and walked away. Ben would be first, but she needed him awake before she killed him.

Loraine went to the sink, and ran cold water into a bowl, then walked across the room to Ben, and threw it on his face. He jerked awake, tearing the IV out of his arm at the same time. A small amount of blood showed in the vein at his hand, eventually turning into a larger spot, dripping onto the floor. He struggled to get himself loose from the plastic ties, looking around the room with the curiosity of where he was. It took him a few seconds to realize who had him, and that he had seen this apartment before. She could see the immediate disappointment, and then fear show in his eyes.

Loraine walked back to the sink, and put the bowl down carefully. She was purposely leaving her back to him, ignoring his stare. She messed with the few dishes that were there for a short time, leaving him alone to think, to wonder what would happen next.

"Loraine?" he started in a quiet voice. He was weak, and it showed in his voice. He could still feel the affects of the sedative they had given him at the hospital. He closed his eyes again, trying to squint the dizziness out of his head. He opened them back up, and tried to sit up on the floor.

"Loraine," he said again. "Let me out of these, please, I'm sure we can talk all of this out."

She continued with her useless moving of dishes, and things around the kitchen. She could hear in his voice that ignoring him was starting to frustrate him. She didn't turn around; she just kept her back to him.

"What do you want?" he said in almost a panicking voice. "What do you want from me, you kept me in that room, and now you have me back here, what do you want?"

She reached in the drawer next to the stove, and pulled out one of her large carving knives. Ben had given her a set just like them for her birthday once. She found the exact match to them at the Wal-Mart, and remembered thinking that he was a cheapskate for buying them for her birthday. Good God, what woman wants a set of carving knives for her birthday? It was one of the things that upset her the most about him; his insensitivity to her wants.

She turned around, and saw that he was trying to scoot his body away towards the elevator shaft. She stepped forward, and stood directly in front of him. She had the knife in her hand, down at her side. He looked up, and saw her and quit trying to move across the floor.

"I'm sick, Loraine, I know that, I can get help and you can help me," his eyes were now pleading at her. "I've changed, I'll change my life, and Aubrey's too."

"Shut-up!" she demanded. She walked over to the window, and looked down at the street. The sun was down now, but dusk was still allowing light to scurry through the streets searching for its final resting place of the night.

She spun back around, and in the same move placed the knife at Ben's throat, "you'll never change, you made our daughter's life a living hell, and now you'll pay for that."

Loraine remained in position until she heard the liquid start to hit the floor, a puddle started to form under Ben where he wet himself from fear, "you pitiful little piss-ant," and she took the knife away from his throat.

She stood back up and walked a few steps away, "do you think I would make it that easy? You won't be so lucky to die that quickly. I want you to feel the fear that Aubrey felt every time you let those bastards in her room."

He looked at her with tears starting to flow down his cheeks, "you're the one that left, not me."

Loraine felt the anger start at the base of her bowels, and build throughout her body. She clenched the knife tight, so tight that she dug her nails into her own hand, drawing blood on each one. She fought with the guilt of leaving Aubrey every day, and every day her feelings for her daughter were put on hold for her own means. She would have to live with that for the rest of her life. She also knew that Aubrey was never going to have to take the abuse of these men again, and for that some of her guilt was lessened. With all that, she was still not going to let this perverted tyrant guilt her into submission. She was originally only going to turn him over to the police, but now things were different, and she had made her decision.

She struggled to regain her composure, and finally felt the anger start to slip back into the depths it came from. She would keep it at the ready in case she needed it again, but for now she wanted to stay calm. Calm would allow her to keep the perspective that she needed.

She was facing Ben while he lay on the floor. He continued to struggle to get the plastic ties off of his hands, ever so slightly, but she could see his effort. There was a sense of confidence in her now that he had never seen. There was never that confidence when they were married, and it took her a long time to build up the courage to even leave him. There wasn't love for a long time in the relationship, only discontent. When she did finally decide to leave him, she saw the man he really was. He made it clear with the threats he gave her after she told him she would take Aubrey with her. He threatened to kill her on the spot, a result that she couldn't let happen. Now it was time for him to know what it was like for her, and for Aubrey. It was time to take him to hell.

Chapter Twenty-Four

Don Breeding and Bob Sammons pulled up outside the loft just behind Ryan. He was still sitting in the car watching the SUV that they had watched pull away from the hospital earlier in the day, and the apartment that she was apparently in. He could see the woman come and go every once in a while in the window, but each time she turned around; her back was to the window so he couldn't see her face. She obviously didn't know he was down there observing her, so he stayed put until the others could arrive. Ryan noticed the car come up behind him, and watched as they parked, and the two occupants get out of the car. There were also two police cars pulling up on the opposite side of the street, just behind the car that she had driven.

Ryan sat and wondered how she had possession of a car that was registered to Mrs. Cranston. Did Cranston lend her the vehicle, or were the two in this together. Cranston was an important woman, and it seemed unlikely that she would be involved in something like this. If she were implicated, it would mean the end of her career in politics. Of course bigger politicians than her had done things that had less affect on the world, and had survived the backlash from the public. There was also the building that had been in the Cranston family for what seemed like ages. The big 'for sale' sign still hung on it, which made Ryan wonder why Cranston would let someone use it.

Maybe Cranston found out about what her husband was doing, and then recruited this lady to help her get rid of all the men at one time. She clearly had a plan, and it was being executed very well so far. He couldn't help but feel that they had put some kinks in it for her, but for the most part she had done what she had set out to do. She had freely and willfully gone around to each of the victims, and killed each one in a way that was, let's say, creative. She had involved others as well, killing the innocent electrical worker, and possibly the old lady in the hospital along with the officer, and the nurse.

Sammons and Don opened his car doors and slid inside. Don sat in the front, and Ryan noticed that he still didn't look as though he was feeling one hundred percent. He was extremely pale, but his cheeks were flushed and red. His hair was messy and still looked as though he had just gotten up from lying down. He handed Ryan a picture, which Ryan looked at with curiosity.

"That's the woman that took Hendrickson and I to the parking garage," he said as he pulled a handkerchief from his pocket, and wiped his lips and forehead. "She's Hendrickson's ex wife, and Aubrey's Mother. Her name is Loraine Bullock; she took her maiden name when she went to work for a doctor not far from UT. That's how she knew how to get through the hospital as well as she did, and how she had access to the drugs that she's given the victims. We also think that's how no one knew who she was. We think when she took the job the only person she knew in the area was Dr. Cranston, and she took measures to insure that she never ran into him."

Sammons filled in some more, "she also had access to Dr. Cranston at the hospital. We're not sure if she actually saw him there, but we're relatively sure that she had some sort of contact with his wife. We think that she went to see Mrs. Cranston after she found out her husband was abusing her daughter. We've sent word to Washington, and apparently Mrs. Cranston is on her way back here. We've got someone at the airport to pick her up. She must have told her what was going on, and the two are in this together. That's the theory anyway."

"So we think she's got Ben Hendrickson in this building, and she's planning on killing him like the rest," said Ryan. "Have we found that guy named Scooter yet? Maybe he can shed some light on some of this."

"They've been to his house, if you want to call it a house," Don said. "He lives in a trailer park near Seymour, and they found a bunch of newspaper boxes in several of the rooms where he'd been stealing quarters out of them, but he wasn't there. We think he must have taken off when he heard of the other deaths. We know he met with Fallon and Massey, just before they were killed, but we haven't seen or heard from him since. I had an all points bulletin put out on him."

Sammons spoke up again from the back seat, "we need to wait for the SWAT team to arrive, and decide then what we're going to do with this. It could get pretty volatile if she's as desperate as we think she is. That was one hell of a gutsy move she made there at the hospital."

"I don't think she's as desperate as you think, Chief. I think she's trying to right a wrong for her daughter, not be a serial killer like we've seen before. Her daughter is on her way down here, she saw the report on television about Hendrickson being found and then taken again. Her friends Mother is driving her down, they should be here any minute."

The three men got out of the car to survey the area. There were two patrol cars parked across the street behind the SUV that Loraine was driving, other than that there were no vehicles on that side of the street. The officer's from the cars were busy taping off the end of the street so others couldn't drive into the area. There were already a handful of people around the yellow police tape. It always astonished Ryan that when the tape went up, it seemed people came from nowhere, and mingled to see whatever it was they were looking for. Ryan could see another officer talking with three women that were trying to gain access to the area. He motioned with his hand to let them through.

The women walked straight over to Ryan and his partner, Aubrey being held around the shoulders of her friend, "do we know if he's in there," Aubrey managed to say in a low voice.

All three men were reluctant to tell her what they believed was going on inside the building. There was every indication that what they believed was in fact true, but without confirmation, Ryan wasn't sure if it was the right thing to do in the situation.

"That's the car the woman was driving that took Don and your father," Ryan told her. "We don't have confirmation on who the woman is, but we have people on the way that will be able to get inside, so we're going to lay low until then. If you ladies would like, you can sit in the car until everything is in place."

"We'll stay out her with you," Sara told them.

Bob Sammons spoke up, "stand over by our car then," he said. "We don't want anything to happen to any of you, and if we need you, we'll come get you."

The three women walked away from the men, and Ryan leaned over to Don, "we need to watch them closely," he whispered. "I don't want them getting out of our sight, none of them."

A black truck with the SWAT team was arriving at the end of the street, it parked where it drove in, and several men climbed out of the back, taking strategic positions all around the area. The commander walked up to Sammons out of earshot to Don and Ryan. They talked for several minutes, and then Sammons came over to Ryan.

"Here's what's going to happen, the SWAT team is going to get into position," he pointed to the adjacent buildings in three different areas, all pointing to the window that Ryan had seen Loraine in. "After they are in position, you're going to try to make contact with her. If she does answer, we'll work it as a negotiation, if not, and the SWAT team can get a clean shot, we'll take her out."

"Listen, Bob, I still think that she only wants to end this whole ordeal with what she started, she's not a threat to the public—"

"It doesn't matter Ryan," Sammons interrupted, "she's killed at least seven people in the last week, maybe eight with the old woman in the ICU, we aren't sure if Ben Hendrickson is alive or dead, and we can't find the final victim that she has obviously vowed to kill. No harm to the public, you're kidding, right?"

"I just don't think we need to rush in there and start shooting, you said it yourself, we don't know if Hendrickson is dead or alive, and who knows who else she has in there, we just need to exercise some caution and work this slower, that's all I'm saying."

The SWAT team was moving through the neighborhood, getting into the positions that the commander had instructed. Each man was carrying the necessary weapons to take care of just about any situation that could arise in the area, each with night vision. Ryan watched as they scurried around to each of the buildings, some going inside, and some just hiding in the alleys. This was turning into the situation that Ryan was afraid of; this was going to be a massacre in a very short time. He turned to say something to Don when he saw Aubrey. She was already at the door to the loft, starting to open the door.

Ryan broke into a run across the street. He arrived just as Aubrey went inside, and he followed quickly behind her. When he caught up with her, he grabbed her arm in the dark hallway.

"What the hell are you doing?" He sternly whispered to her. "We have to go back outside, and let the proper people handle this."

"I'm going up there, I want to know what's going on," she said back to him.

Ryan looked at her in the dark, trying to come up with a solution that would make her go back outside. The two were standing next to the area the elevator would go up; just down the hallway was a stairway that led up to the floors above. It was dark, and hard to see if the stairs were even still there. The building was in terrible shape on this floor, trash scattered the hallway along with liquid, and pieces of food that was discarded during some part of the day. The walls were painted with graffiti and curse words. He looked back at Aubrey just as a loud thud sounded over the top of them, followed by a gruesome moan.

Ryan drew his weapon, and motioned for Aubrey to get behind him. He looked up the elevator shaft, and saw that the lift was on the floor above them. Light trickled between the cracks in the floor of the elevator exposing the well-used portion of the floor. He wondered if anyone could have the courage to ride in something as worn out as it was. There would be no way for them to get the lift down without someone hearing them.

Then another thud on the floor, this time it was followed by a cry of inflicted pain, and sobbing. Ryan could hear a woman's voice almost yelling at someone, it wasn't loud enough to understand, but it sounded angry.

Outside, Don motioned for all the others to stay in place, not to follow Ryan into the building. He stood there with Sammons next to him, the two men stared at each other for a few moments, then Don spoke up, "he's got himself into something here I hope he can get out of."

Sammons nodded in agreement, and got on his radio to the SWAT Commander, explaining that things had changed, they now had a fellow officer inside the building, and no one was to shoot.

Chapter Twenty-Five

Loraine stood over Ben with the knife in her hand; it was pointed down, not at his face or his chest, but at his groin. She stood directly over him, staring, with her legs on each side of his body. She didn't say anything, only breathed heavily as she tried to get herself into the right frame of mind that she needed to finish him off.

He was sobbing fully now, and tried with all his might to get out of the restraints she had put him in. He couldn't move, only twist back and forth.

She thought that he looked pitiful, sprawled on the floor, crying like a baby. She wondered if he ever sat in his filthy chair in the living room of his house, and thought about Aubrey upstairs with those men, doing things that he sent them up to do. The more she thought about it, the angrier she became.

"Stop trying to get away, it won't do any good, you're not going anywhere, this is your final trip anywhere." She took her foot, and pressed against his scrotum. He screamed, loud and long.

Loraine removed her foot and stepped to his side, "did that hurt, think about it, did it hurt the big man real bad?" She said in a baby tone. "You have no idea what hurt is yet," then she took the knife, placed it on his belt and cut the leather as if it were ribbon.

She stood up again, and for the second time, Ben pissed on himself, he was terrified, and she knew it. She bent over, placed the knife on the top of his wet pants, and split the zipper with one swift slash. His pants popped open exposing his now soaked underwear. She ran the knife down his shorts and stopped at the base of his penis.

"You can say you're sorry Ben, you can even scream, and plead for mercy. You can swear that you'll change your life, but nothing is going to save you, nothing saved your precious friends did it?" She took the knife and put a clean slice all the way from the crotch to the waistband of his shorts.

She slowly moved the knife back and forth on his skin, the sharp blade taking small pieces of hair. The knife drew slim rivers of blood that trickled down both sides of his hips. He shuddered with the thought of her cutting him. There wasn't a lot of pain, and he was too terrified to feel the knife cutting him, only the feel of the cold blade moving slowly down his belly. Mentally he knew he couldn't take much more. He started to get dizzy, and prayed to himself to pass out; he thought maybe he might have said it out loud. He tried to squirm out of the ties one more time, this time causing Loraine to accidentally cut deeper than she intended. This time he winced in pain, and just like before, the ties did not move. He was still bound.

Now the pain was coming in waves, shooting through his body. What he couldn't feel before came crashing through the barrier of shock, hitting him like a hammer. He looked down at his naked midsection, and saw that she had cut him deep enough that blood now covered him in a deep red puddle, making a small puddle effect in his belly button.

"Now look what you made me do," she moved the knife away for a moment. "I think I cut you a little bit too deep, didn't I?" She put her hand over her mouth, as if she had made a mistake with a child.

Even with the pain, Ben thought that the act was getting a little annoying. If she was going to kill him, he wished she would get it done. It looked like she was enjoying herself, as she smiled when she danced the knife around the wounds she made. She looked as though she wanted him suffering as long as she could make him. The only thing that overpowered his humiliation was the pain he was feeling from the new cuts, and the previous wounds she had inflicted on him.

She reached down, and grabbed him around the balls, lifting them high enough that it made him wince. The knife was positioned at the base with the blade touching slightly. Loraine wasn't looking at the knife, or what she was about to cut; she was staring directly into his eyes. Her stare was piercing and judgmental, and he could tell by her look that it was the stare of someone on the brink of insanity.

"I hope you're terrified, Ben. You remember as I kill you, the innocence you stole from our daughter. I hope that when this is all over, and you're dead in front of me, that I get to watch as the devil himself comes to take you to hell!"

With one swift movement she brought the knife upward taking with it his manhood. The blood squirted upward onto Loraine's legs, and up around her arms. There was no scream, only a quiet muffled gasp as his head went back, and his eyes rotated up into the sockets. She straightened up into a standing position holding her prize in her hands.

She moved off of him, and looked down one last time. There was no movement, only Ben on the floor, blood flowing out of him, his face was now calm, and his eyes closed.

The ringleader, the man that had put her daughter through hell, was finally dead. She dropped the pieces that she had sliced off, and hovered over him, watching, taking all pleasure and no guilt in his death.

"Don't move!" rang out behind her, startling her, and making her spin around to see who had yelled.

The shot hit her right above her left breast, stinging into her entire body. She didn't fall; she only looked at the sudden wetness coming from the wound. She raised her head, and saw Ryan a few feet away from her with the gun still at the ready. She heard someone scream, and she noticed Aubrey standing by the man that had just pulled the trigger on her. She fell to her knees on the floor next to Ben Hendrickson's body.

Aubrey ran to her mother, falling next to her as she reached for her and held her tight. Loraine fell into her arms, letting her body slide into a hug from her daughter. Aubrey looked at her through tearful eyes. A tear from Aubrey, landed on Loraine's cheek, and mixed with her own. The two women looked at each other, both with faces of disbelief.

"Aubrey looked up at Ryan, "you shot her you son of a bitch, why'd you shoot her?"

She looked into the eyes of her mother in her arms, "Momma, you'll be all right, just stay with me."

"Aubrey," Loraine took her hand, and put it on Aubrey's cheek. "You're so beautiful, and now you can live your life the way you want. I told you I'd come back, I'm just sorry it took so long to do it. Can you ever forgive me?"

Aubrey hugged her mother hard, and stroked her hair, "yes, I forgive you, now we can go home together, and no one can hurt either one of us," as she hugged her tighter.

Loraine looked up at her beautiful Aubrey Lenore, taking in every aspect of her face; the tears were flowing down her cheek, and landing in big drops. They were the tears of sadness, but Loraine felt happiness in her heart. Happiness that it was finally over, she had almost done what she set out to do, and the only one that still loved her was holding her tight, comforting her in the final moments of her life. She thought that it had to be what heaven was like, the love pouring on you from above. Her eyes opened wide, and she sighed one last time as the blackness of death took her, with her last vision of Aubrey, stroking her hair.

Several officers of the Knoxville Police Department were now coming up into the apartment from the stairwell that Ryan and Aubrey had just come from. All of them had guns drawn as they checked each room in the loft. They ran to Loraine's side, kicking the knife that she had dropped when she fell out of the way. Don tried to take Aubrey from Loraine's side, but she wouldn't let go of her mother. Ryan touched him on the shoulder, and motioned for him to leave her alone for a moment. Sammons walked over, and patted Ryan on the back.

It seemed to Ryan right then that no one won in this situation. A woman that was trying to right a wrong had just slipped away, and took with her all the hopes of a young girl. It was a night none of them would ever forget. He walked over to Don, and the two men headed out to the waiting cars downstairs.

Chapter Twenty-Six

Ryan and Don sat in the car watching as the Knox County Coroner took the bodies out of the loft. The lights from the activity had brought people outside to watch the spectacle of another crime in the city. The two men didn't feel any relief, only sadness for what had happened. Some of the spectators were starting to leave the area, but amongst the departing public were two people walking toward the car, one was a woman with her hands cuffed behind her. At her side was Bob Sammons, escorting her to the two waiting detectives in the car. Ryan stepped out with Don close behind, as the two got closer, Ryan could see that the woman was Evelyn Cranston.

"We picked her up at the airport when she came back tonight from Washington. She told us everything on the way over, how she lent the car to Loraine, rented her the loft, and helped her with at least one of the murders."

"I didn't know she was going to kill them all," she said in a half-hearted voice. "I just wanted her to take care of both of our husbands, that's all. I had nothing to do with any of the other murders."

Sammons handed her to the waiting officer, "take her to the station, I'll be back there soon." They walked away in the array of flashing bulbs from the media that had gathered.

Don watched as they walked to the car and she was put in the back seat, "what a waste, all around if you ask me. So many lives affected by such stupidity."

Ryan stayed deep in his thoughts as he watched the car drive away, with what many thought would have one of the more promising careers in politics. It was hard to blame her or Loraine Hendrickson for their crimes. The men they either killed, or aided in the murder, were the worst known to anyone. Loraine felt the need to take care of something that she didn't feel society would accomplish, and to tell the truth, the world was probably a better place for her actions. It still baffled him why someone would resort to selling his daughter into prostitution, but he figured if you could understand it, you could probably do it. He was brought out of his thoughts by a tap on his shoulder from Don.

Aubrey was being brought out of the building with another female detective. Her hair was a mess, and the crying made her look older than she was. Her friend Amy and Amy's mother were at her side, trying to hug her, but looking more like they were holding her up. She walked past Ryan and Don, without a word, only a quick look of despair. Both men just looked at the ground with sorrow and disgust.

"She's gonna to be ok," Sammons, said. "You didn't have any choice Ryan; all of us would have done the same thing."

"Doesn't make it any easier," Ryan said, "I guess I should have waited until she turned all the way around."

"There's no reason to place that guilt on yourself, she had a knife in her hand, you didn't have any way of knowing what she would've done, especially under the circumstances. It was a good shoot," he turned, started to walk away, but turned.

"Listen, you guys go home tonight, and take tomorrow off; you both deserve it. Make sure you get the reports filed as soon as you get back."

Ryan watched as the three women walked away, Aubrey and Amy, both fingering the necklace they wore, then he turned to Don, "he's right, it looks like most of this is cleaned up, lets get out of here, this one made me tired, Don, very, very, tired."

There were only a few lights from the police cars remaining on the street as lights from the city reflected off the snow into the night sky. It would be another cold day, but it looked clear anyway, no more snow in sight. Hopefully a better day was ahead.

Inside the building, Scooter Sampson looked around the small room he still lay in. The ropes were still around his wrists, and ankles, and he couldn't see anything in the darkness. He had heard the noise outside the door, but the tape on his mouth prevented him from yelling. He blinked continuously as he tried to see anything around, or inside the room.

It sounded like shots were fired, and he could hear plenty of people in the house that could find him if they looked. He stopped moving around as much, he would need his strength later. Staying put would be the best thing; eventually someone would come to the small door, and let him out.

He got excited as he heard someone walking over to the door, and trying the lock, they also tried the lock in the handle, jiggling it several times, "this is locked from the outside, should we try to see what's inside," said the voice.

"Na," said another voice, "if it ain't open, just leave it, they'll probably end up tearing this place down anyway, when they do, whatever is in there will be found or buried in the rubble."

Scooter tried to move but the ropes prevented him from going anywhere. He frantically tried to bang his legs on the floor, but got only dull thuds. He yelled as loud as he could, but it came out as a low muffled blubbering through the tape that covered his mouth. He saw under the door as the shadows went the other way, the sound of footsteps walking out of the range of his rescue. The light outside the door went out, and he heard the elevator start up, and lumber its way to the bottom floor. He was alone again, in the dark with no hope of anyone coming into the small room. He began to cry, tears hitting the cold floor, he could feel the panic coming to him in stages, but without an outlet, the feelings were just trapped inside, much like he was now trapped. He slowly realized that she had put him in this small hell that she wanted him in, that if she had intended to kill him, she may have failed in that attempt, but in her failure, her victory was clear.

He lay there for a moment and looked around in the dark with tears streaming down his face, "help me," he mumbled under the tape, "help me, please."

There was no answer, only a deafening silence.

Printed in the United States
200500BV00004B/217/A

9 781604 416206